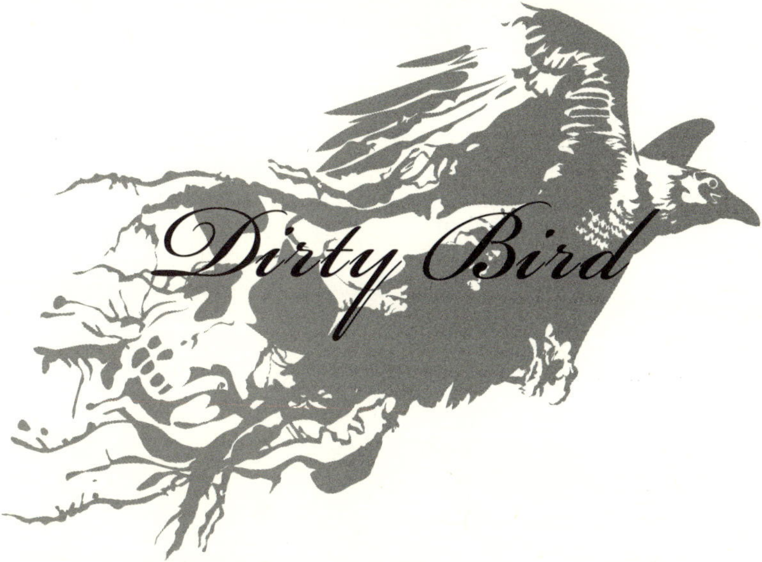

Dirty Bird

a novel by

Keir Lowther

Copyright © 2012 Keir Lowther
All rights reserved

Tightrope Books
167 Browning Trail
Barrie, Ontario. L4N 5E7
www.tightropebooks.com

Editor: Robyn Read
Copyeditors: Myna Wallin and James Tanner
Cover Design: Deanna Janovski
Book design and typography: Dawn Kresan

Printed and bound in Canada

We thank the Canada Council for the Arts and the Ontario Arts Council for their support of our publishing program.

   Canada Council   Conseil des Arts
     for the Arts   du Canada

   ONTARIO ARTS COUNCIL
     CONSEIL DES ARTS DE L'ONTARIO

Library and Archives Canada Cataloguing in Publication

Lowther, Keir
    Dirty bird / Keir Lowther.

ISBN 978-1-926639-52-9

    I. TITLE.

PS8623.O93D57 2012   C813'.6   C2012-904964-6

…With all its sham, drudgery, and broken dreams, it is still a beautiful world.

—Desiderata by Max Ehrmann

1

Knock, knock on the door and I got up from the sofa and walked from the living room through the kitchen and opened the door and who was there but my dead cousin Miles. His head was shaved like it was on the day of his wake and funeral. It was like that because when he hit his head it began to swell like a growing balloon that was about to pop. In order to relieve the swelling the doctors shaved his head and cut it open. Mum said it did relieve the swelling but he died anyway.

I wasn't surprised to see him standing in front of me, smelling of dirt and worms, and told him so. I also told him how much I loved him, and hugged him, but he squirmed out of my hug like a worm and just stood there.

I asked him to take off his black boots. They were covered in dirt and they were getting Mum and her boyfriend Jody's white kitchen floor dirty. I didn't mean to take away from his coming back to life but I wanted to keep the floor clean because we just moved in with Jody and he told me that if I made a mess of his place he would make sure I wound up in the nuthouse. I knew all about the nuthouse because Miles had lived there for a while. I had gone to visit him a few times. Once I even brought him a Happy Meal.

"Take off your boots," I said again. I told him where Jody would send me if I made a mess of his place. Miles didn't seem to care though. I just hoped that Mum and Jody wouldn't care either under the circumstances.

"How've you been?" I said.

He grunted and I knew that meant he was fine. He grunted again and I knew that meant he was kind of tired. I had other questions and so we just stood there, face to face in the kitchen, and I asked him more. It turned out that he broke through his casket and dug through the earth, eating worms along the way because it took him almost the whole year he was buried to dig himself out. When he got near the surface he dug and punched really hard to break through the earth that was cold and icy like a frozen pizza. Then he walked from the graveyard, past Grampy's, past the peeing church, to my house.

"I'm glad you came to see me first," I said.

He replied with a bunch of grunts that sounded like a rap song, but I knew what they meant. When he got diagnosed with his disease he felt like a rotten potato, all right on the outside but a dark smelly mush on the inside and even though people couldn't always see the mush they treated him differently except for me. He felt bad that he didn't get a chance to say bye before he left for Calgary and died and that was why he came to see me first.

Miles died on December 18th, over a year before the day he knocked on my door. That day doesn't matter though, because really he died about a month before that. He was brain dead and it was just a formality, them keeping him alive on that life machine. I guess he only had two percent brainpower and so even if he lived and was able to breathe for himself, he would've been as swift as a cucumber or carrot. That's what Mum said. That explained the grunting.

Miles was from PEI like me, but when he died he was out in Calgary. I guess he was off his pills and he only told Grampy he was going out west an hour before he left. Mum said it wasn't Grampy's fault for letting him go. Miles was twenty, a grown man. Grampy couldn't make him take his pills and he couldn't make him stay in PEI with us. Besides, Miles could've just as easily died washing dishes, Mum said. All it takes is a slip. What I took from this was that I would be a grown man soon too because Miles was only eight years older than me.

I hoped the day Miles died was a good day for him. It probably was because he just arrived in Calgary and his wallet was full of money from working all summer at a fish restaurant. He washed dishes and took out the garbage and he was so good at that that they even let him cut onions and potatoes and carrots. He worked until the restaurant closed at the end of the season. For the first time since his mind problem was diagnosed he was able to hold down a job. The work wasn't great, he told me, but earning money was. He didn't know if he wanted to be a doctor or a math-man because of his mind problem, and that's all I'll say on that. Except that they think I got a mind problem too.

The first thing Miles did when he got out to Calgary was find a hotel room and the second thing he did was go to his favourite strip club with bikini in its name. And I bet the women liked having him around because he was the coolest person I knew and was quiet most of the time except for when he would say out loud the raps he was always listening to on his headphones. So I bet he just sat and drank a pop and maybe shared a rap or two with the girls while he watched them take off their clothes and dance and spread their legs, showing off their buck-naked birds. He spent the day at the club and when it was getting dark he found a pay phone and called Grampy. He missed all of us and wanted to come home. He died before that could happen though. At least there wasn't any pain, Mum said. It was just lights out.

I looked at Miles and told him that I loved him and missed him and that I just went over his final day in my mind. I told him that I had questions about it but that they didn't matter anymore since he was alive right there in front of me. I tried to hug him again but he dodged it by squirming like a worm again. I guess he spent too much time with the worms and was beginning to act like one. I asked him if he would like to have a seat in the armchair in the living room since he was tired. He grunted, and so I took him by the hand and led him into the living room and took him right over to the seat. I pushed him on top of it and he fell into its coziness. He turned his head over to the side and looked out the big picture window at the sun.

He grunted and I closed the curtains. Then I asked him what I wanted to ask him since I opened the door and saw it was him.

"What's it like to die?"

He didn't answer me. I thought there might be dirt in his ears but then he grunted. Once he started grunting he didn't stop and I just listened. When I thought he was finished I said, "Wow—"

But he wasn't finished, and he looked away from the curtains and into my eyes and grunted and I knew that he found death lonely and that was why he'd come back. He smiled for the first time that day. His eyes were dark like flies and his teeth were the colour of poop and it was the scariest smile I'd ever seen.

It wasn't long after that Mum and Jody came home from eating. They were angry about all the dirt on the floor. Mum swatted me in the butt and Jody cursed at me like a rapper (though he didn't say anything about sending me to the nuthouse) and when I told them that Miles made the mess Mum's body started shaking like the washing machine.

"Trina, come on," Jody said, and he grabbed her by the shoulders and took her to their room. Even with the door closed I heard the yelling and crying. Then the bed started squeaking. Soon there was silence, and I asked Miles if he wanted to go spy on the neighbours or something. But his eyes were closed. He was asleep. I decided not to wake him. He hadn't rested in almost a year.

2

I stuck my hand down my pants and rubbed my bird. It started to grow and soon enough it was hard as a tree branch. I was about to go to the couch and lie down and look through some of my favourite pictures I found in the shoebox hidden in the wall in the basement when I saw out the window a crow in a tree. The crow was doing nothing really, maybe deciding if it was going to eat my garbage. Then suddenly it turned its head and its black eyes stared into mine. Not even my skin or hair could keep it from looking into my mind and knowing my secrets. What I did once for five dollars. How hard I laughed after I called the cops and told them that Dad stole a car and was driving it around like it was his own. The crow saw that I would do almost anything to get Mum to myself and it also saw my hard hairy bird. I knew it wanted to come perch on it so I pulled up my pants. It flew over to the power line in front of my neighbour Winston's place instead. And I disappeared into my room where I took my bird out again while I looked at some pictures.

Later that day I went outside. I walked across the grass and to the top of the ditch. The sun hurt my eyes. Sweat came out of me, making my armpits stink like old apple juice, so I dropped to the grass and rolled down to the bottom of the ditch. When I stopped moving I was dizzy, but I was in the shade. The sun could no longer reach me but the voices of the kids on the street did. They were on the road, right in front of my house, perched on their bikes like crows on a branch. Their bikes were shiny and colourful and the tires were full of air. My bike used to be green but now it was rusty and the tires were as flat as the road. I wanted to get them filled so that I would be able to drive around like the other kids but there was nobody around to help me with that. Dad was gone to jail and Jody was away flying planes and Mum was busy giving people food or watching TV. There were yummy hot pea hamburgers where she worked and I'd mash my peas into the soggy bread and gravy when she brought me a cold one home.

I laid there in the ditch and the kids called me names.

"Shut up," I said.

"You asked for it, dumb ass," one of them said.

Pinecones and rocks rained down on me. First they missed and I was smiling one of those McDonald's smiles. It was free. Then a rock like a bird came down from the sky and bit me on the lip. I started to cry, the silent crying, and then I tasted blood. That's when the shaking and hard crying began, and the wanting the kids to be gone or dead.

"Retard," one of them yelled. The voice was high like a girl's but I knew it was one of the boys. My voice was deep, deep like Dad's. I didn't like Dad but I missed him right then because if he was here he would tell those kids to fuck off and that's exactly what they would do. The last time I saw Dad was the night the cops knocked on our door. Mum let them in and they walked past me trying not to laugh and over to Dad. He was making cigarettes at the coffee table.

"Just let me finish," Dad said.

And as one of the cops went to say something to the other cop, Dad lifted the coffee table and threw it in his face. He took off running down the hall and out the side door. It was dark and he ran across the field and by the time the cops were outside they couldn't see him. The next morning they found him in town walking down a street in his socks. He went to jail and I was happy because I thought Mum was all mine. Then she met Jody.

I wasn't too smart in school but I did know that I should keep my telling on Dad a secret. And I did a good job of that until my mind was broken into by the crow that was a criminal like Dad and deserved to be in jail. I thought all this and then it stopped raining rocks and pinecones. I heard an engine growl. The growling kept growing louder and at first I thought it was my belly because I was hungry. But then it got too loud for that.

Right then I saw something move so I turned my head. The same crow was now in the ditch with me, just a few feet down. Its hair was oily and shiny like my black hair and I expected to see white stuff in it, like in mine, but I didn't. The crow looked over at me and I was scared because its black bubble eyes stared into mine. It was like what I felt in the morning, my brain bucknaked. But I think the crow was bored of looking into me and it flapped its wings. It rose out of the ditch. Soon it stopped rising but its wings kept flapping and it was looking to where the kids and their shiny bikes probably were. I grabbed a rock for a weapon and crawled up the ditch to see what was happening.

There were four kids and four shiny bikes standing up on kickstands. Three of the kids were turned around watching the garbage truck at work, and the fourth was staring at the crow, the crow at him. I thought he would have no secrets because he drove a shiny bike and lived in a big house with probably a milkshake maker. I thought he would throw a rock at the crow and the crow would fly away but his eyes went wide and his lips shook. His face shook like mine when I tasted my own blood and I was happy for lots of reasons but mainly because I wasn't the only one who was broken into.

I guess one of the kids noticed me peeking and something hit me in the shoulder. It hurt. The crow flew like an airplane to the garbage bag I forgot to take out, leaving me alone at the top of the ditch. I threw my weapon in the air and rolled back into the ditch. When I undizzied I heard crying, this loud crying that came, I thought, from the boy whose mind was robbed of its secrets. The rain stopped again and soon the crying wasn't as loud. Soon I heard no crying at all. The kids must all be gone, I thought. And I was right, because when I finally left the ditch that afternoon after the taxi dropped Mum off in our driveway, they were gone. I followed her into the house and she set a brown bag on the table.

"There's some fries for you, " she said.

There was another brown bag in her hand, and I guessed there was a bottle in it. A bottle of what, I didn't know, but I figured there was a picture of a pirate on it and it gave her sour breath. Mum left the kitchen.

Just let me tell you, those cold hard fries were no hot pea hamburger but they were better than coleslaw. I ate them all. Then I went looking for Mum and found her lying on the couch, holding a different bottle with a bull not a pirate. She was watching one of her soaps on the TV. I said to her what was on my mind.

"Tomorrow can you take me to McDonald's to get a Happy Meal?" I said.

"Not now," she said.

"But—"

"We'll talk about this later."

"When later?"

"Later, like when I say it's later."

"Crows are dirty birds."

"I'm missing my show. And don't think I didn't notice the garbage."

I was tired after a day in the sun and went to my room and lay down. I closed my eyes. I tried to sleep but I couldn't because my mind was too busy remembering what happened after it stopped raining rocks and pinecones before Mum got home.

I had been sitting in the sunlight, watching bugs crawl around the yellow smelly flowers that stained my hands. I heard somebody walk towards me. I turned my head. It was Winston, my neighbour with the one tired eye and crumpled hand that couldn't move because it got an electric shock.

"How're ya doing there?" he said.

"Good," I said.

"Playing with flowers?"

"Yeah," I said, and rolled from my tummy to my back and looked up at him. He looked bad, almost deader than my cousin Miles the day he got buried in the ground.

Winston was old.

"Don't play with them too much. You don't want to go girly on us."

"Yeah," I said, but I didn't know what he meant by girly.

"I'm on the hunt for something," he said, and walked lopsidedly over to the metal tunnel under the driveway. He ducked down and reached his good hand into it. He grunted and his hand searched for a while. The sun got covered by a cloud and the whole ditch went dark. A fly buzzed in my ear. Then he came out with it, a jam jar filled with stuff that looked like water but I knew it wasn't water because he could have got water from the tap.

"I've got to stash it somewhere, or else I'll drink it all in one go," he said.

He stuck the jar under his arm and twisted it open with his good hand. He drank half the jar in one mouthful, and said, "The problem's that I can't always remember where I have it stashed."

He stood there leaning on the side that didn't get shocked and staring at me. Then the crow landed in the ditch. The crow was all sleek like a Trans Am, probably full because for most of the afternoon it had eaten the garbage that I forgot to take out. I noticed the crow was staring at Winston, Winston at the crow. And I wished I could know what was in Winston's head. But then I thought maybe I was better off not knowing because the stuff in my head was hard enough to keep straight. I knew he had a hairy-faced wife who never left the house—I saw her at the window a few times. I also knew that last fall he ate his pet pig that he kept in a cage in his backyard. I knew this because he came over to the house and gave Jody a bag of bloody pork chops. That was what we had the next night for supper, so I guess we helped eat his pet pig too.

I couldn't tell if Winston was bothered by the crow or not, because his face stayed the same the whole time the crow stared at him. They were like statues in front of buildings and it was a while before the crow turned and walked up the ditch.

Winston finished the stuff in the jar and burped. His eye twitched. "Fuckin dirty birds," he said, and he threw the jar at the crow, hitting it in the head. The crow fell over on its side. It kicked its legs like it was riding a bike. Then it went still.

"They're always at your garbage, the shit you just want to throw out," he said.

He went and picked up the empty jar and walked like an old man back to his place.

I lay there and watched the bird, hoping it wouldn't get up. It didn't, and its beady eyes weren't intense anymore. They were glassy like the jam jar. I went back to watching bugs crawl around the flowers.

Mum got home soon after that and I stood up. She was getting out of a cab when I took another look down at the crow. It knew all my secrets and I wanted to make sure it was dead. I stepped on its head. I put all my weight on one foot and I felt and heard its beak and bones break. I smiled as I ran after Mum, hoping there was food in the brown bag.

3

It was raining these big drops of water and Mum was lying on the couch.

"My poor feet," she said. "They worked all day."

"I'll rub your feet," I said.

"No thanks. Your hands go places they shouldn't go."

I giggled.

She drank from the bottle that gave her sour breath.

Jody was away flying planes, and she was cranky and her breath was sour the whole time he was gone. One of the times Jody was away she had a sleepover with another man. In the morning he called me Champ. I liked that name better than my own. I thought of him as my friend, though Mum told me never to talk about him in front of Jody because he wouldn't understand her having a sleepover.

Before I left the living room I walked to the armchair and fixed my bed blanket.

It was nighttime and raining and I put on my coat and went outside. I liked rain and night together because it meant everybody would stay inside and I would have the street to myself. Our street zigzagged like a snake with ten houses on it. There was Ada and John and us at the tail of the snake, Georgina and

Winston at its curving middle, and Michelle, the girl with big coconuts, at its scaly head. There were also some other houses that belonged to the kids with shiny bikes, but I was too afraid of what they'd do to me if they caught me staring in their windows.

The rain was warm and I started the night off at the scaly head of the snake. I looked in John's windows but there were no lights on and I figured he wasn't home. His arms were big and covered in pictures and he drove a motorbike. That's where I figured he was, riding his bike, because that was what he always did in the summer. John was the coolest old guy I ever met. Mum liked him too because he was the man she had the sleepover with. I thought about asking Mum if I could have my own sleepover. The person I really wanted to ask was Michelle, the girl on my street with big coconuts, but I knew I couldn't ask her until I got my bed blanket back from the chair. And I couldn't get my bed blanket back until I figured out what to do with what was under it.

I walked across the street to Ada's. All the lights were on in her house and there was music and it seemed like she was having a party. I crawled between two bushes and stood up next to the window and saw that the only person at the party was Ada. She sat in a chair with a pop-up footrest, smoking. People sang on the TV. Her hair was short like a man's. What I loved most about Ada was her smile. It was a nice shade of yellow like there was a campfire in her mouth.

Ada lived by herself now because her husband died in the spring. I watched them rush him into an ambulance and a day later I heard Jody say the old prick was finally dead. Jody told Mum he wasn't too nice to Ada. She did all of the cooking and cleaning and even mowed the lawn. All she ever got in return were bruises and tongue-lashings because she would never know what it was like to go to war. "The old prick could sour the sweetest of apples," Jody said to Mum after he learned Ada's husband died. Mum laughed. One of the only things I liked about Jody was that he could make her laugh because she had one of the best laughs I ever heard. It made me laugh too even if I was in my unfunniest mood.

Through her window I watched people sing on the TV. Ada sometimes sang along and she liked her TV loud so I heard everything clear like I was in my own living room. There was some good singing and I felt the music get inside of me, filling me like a burp that needed to get out. I didn't know the words but I didn't let that stop me from singing.

Ada turned her head towards the window when she heard me. I ducked. I pressed my hand over my mouth and waited for her to come outside. The door never opened and I searched in the ground for worms. I'd been wondering about their taste ever since my cousin Miles survived on them for over a year. All I found were rocks and dirt and used smokes. I looked again in her window. There was no more singing on the TV, just talking, and Ada's eyes were closed and her hand hung over the side of the chair, a smoke still between her fingers. It didn't surprise me that she even smoked in her sleep. I never saw her not smoking and I wondered what they tasted like, if they were like a stick of chocolate and that was why everybody liked them so much. I was lost in my mind wondering and when I looked again for the smoke between her fingers it was gone. It wasn't in her mouth either and that was when I noticed the puddle of fire on the rug. It was small and cute like a kitten and I was excited down through my belly and legs. It wasn't every day I got to see fire.

The fire even acted like a kitten. It made all sorts of moves like rolling on its back and kicking its legs in the air. It also chased its tail and climbed her chair and it grew to be the size of a cat. But it wasn't lazy like the cats I knew. It spread and grew and soon it was the size of a lion. It had her cornered and I was excited to see what would happen next.

Ada coughed but she didn't wake up. She was probably deep in a dream where she was up on stage singing into a camera and people like me were singing along at home in front of our TVs. That would be a nice dream.

The fire pounced on her footrest. It quickly spread to her slipper and that was enough to wake her. She coughed hard and it took her a second to realize what was happening. When she did she kicked off her slippers and stood on the chair. Her mouth opened wide and it looked like she was going to yell for help. Instead she grabbed the phone on the table next to the chair. I felt the heat through the glass and tasted smoke as Ada screamed her name and address into the phone while the fire climbed over the side of the chair. The arm was in flames when she looked out the window. Her eyes moved to me and they opened even wider.

"Help," she said. "For god's sake I see you. Help."

She held the phone and yelled at me as the fire jumped onto her robe. She kicked her legs like she was dancing and her mouth was open, screeching like a singer at the loudest best part of a song. But it felt different now that she knew I was there. Less like a party.

Before I crawled out from between the bushes she yelled my name. I was surprised she even knew my name because we never spoke. She only ever smiled at me.

I ran home in the rain. Our street smelled of barbeque and I was hungry and I knew there was food in the fridge. Before flying off into the sky Jody filled the fridge and cupboards with groceries and that was one of the only other things I liked about him.

When I was in my driveway I heard glass smash. I knew it came from Ada's. I climbed the stairs and went inside.

"Is that you?" Mum said.

"Yeah," I said.

"I'll let you rub my feet, but only my feet," she said. "Understand?"

I walked into the living room. By the sound of her voice I knew her breath was nice and sour.

"Yeah," I said.

"You're soaked, and you smell like smoke," she said. "Jesus, you're not smoking?"

"No," I said. "What makes a party good?"

"I guess if everybody has a good time," she said, laughing. "Now give my feet a little rub."

I rubbed and she moaned and I was happy. I forgot all about Ada, up until I heard the sirens and saw the flashing lights on our street. I looked over at Mum. She was asleep. She slept and I rubbed her feet and legs until the sun rose. I was tired but I was trying to decide whether or not it was a good party. I liked rain and music and fire, especially together, but I also liked Ada and her smile. It warmed me like a campfire.

In the morning there was a knock on the door. Mum's eyes opened. There was another knock and she got up off the sofa. I followed her.

"Hello," said the policeman. His uniform was blue like at McDonald's and he was holding a notepad. "I need to ask you and your son a few questions," he said.

Before Mum could say anything I ran back through the kitchen to the living room and made sure there wasn't anything sticking out from under my bed blanket.

"Can't get the kid to clean his room but he'll tidy out here," she said.

"Is it all right if I come in," he asked.

"Sure, whatever," Mum said, stepping away from the door and taking a seat at the kitchen table. She was still wearing her work uniform, a wrinkly green dress with her name on it. And her yellow hair was flat on her head like it hadn't woken up yet but I could tell the officer liked the look of her. Everybody liked the look of her. She told me once that that was her problem. "I'm just a face, not a voice," she said. I told her I didn't understand what that meant but that she was the most beautiful mum I ever saw. She frowned.

"I'm sure you already know what happened last night," he said.

"What are you talking about?" Mum said.

He told her that there was a fire on the street. That he was sorry to tell her this but Ada was dead. They found her outside her house in the bushes.

"A fire in the bushes?"

"No, in her house. She tried to escape the fire by jumping through her living room window."

Mum's face went white and she said, "Ada was a sweet woman. God."

"I'm here to find out if your son was home last night," he said.

Mum looked over at me and I could tell she was confused.

"What do you mean?" she said.

"Was your son home all night?" he said.

She nodded.

"Mind if I ask him?" he said.

"Fill your boots," she said.

I knew he wanted me to fill his boots with the truth and Mum wanted me to fill them with lies. Since I was having trouble deciding what to say, I didn't want to disappoint Mum but I was afraid of the police, I stayed quiet and was glad there were no crows around.

"Is everything all right with him?" the policeman said.

Mum explained.

He nodded and said to Mum, "Okay, it's just that in the 911 transcript from last night, well, I'll read you Ada's final words." He opened his notepad and read, "Help. For God's sake I see you. Help. Travis…don't leave me."

Mum's face went from white to purple as if it was covered by one big ugly birthmark like Jody's.

"I don't know what to say," she said. "He was home all night with me."

"What time did you go to bed?" he said.

"One, two."

He wrote in his notebook, thanked us for our time and said that he may have a few more questions and would be in touch. Before leaving he looked down at my sneakers. They were covered in mud from Ada's garden and he asked Mum what size my feet were.

Mum had one voice for the truth and another for lies. I didn't know what size she would say but I already knew what voice she would use.

When the policeman left Mum walked over to the cupboards. She pulled out a box of cereal and said, "Whatever you had to do with it, I don't want to know. Nobody really wants to know, understand?"

"But the policeman wants to know," I said.

"It's his job to think he does, but he doesn't."

She walked past me with the box of cereal into the living room. I stood in the kitchen. I yawned. The sky was grey and I felt scared of the future like probably Ada did, fire cooking her like a hotdog.

4

One day Trina's husband decided he had had enough: the working in a warehouse, the sweating eight to four, the soggy sandwiches for lunch and a stiff back, the stench of hard work with him day and night for a small cheque every two weeks. He quit his job and got mixed up with car thieves. He didn't do the actual stealing, he was the one who delivered them from PEI to Moncton where the actual work was done. New paint, new numbers, new cars. They were from a small island. There weren't any secrets on an island that size and she kept telling him that but there were two voices in his head. Hers and the money's. Of course he listened to the money but just like she warned him, word spread and he was arrested. For his part he was sentenced to seven years in Dorchester. Besides some of his parents' old furniture, all he left Trina with was a kid, bills, and crabs.

She knew staying on top of the kid and the bills was going to be a struggle. The crabs, they did a number on her. Not the actual crabs. Trips to the doctor and drugstore cured that itch. It was what they meant, the fact that he probably got them on one of those trips to Moncton. Her deep in worry about him getting home safe, him deep inside some slut. She got heavy into the rye. Her nights were cloudy and wet. Her days were long and dry unless she called in sick for work, then they were wet like the nights and in her line of work—she was a waitress—they didn't pay her to be sick and so her cheques got smaller as her bills piled up.

Her nephew died.

She got fired from her job.

She pawned everything but the TV.

Notices of overdue accounts began arriving in the mail as often as letters declaring she had won millions. When they stopped the phone calls started. She told Travis not to answer the phone. She hardly answered it anymore, but one of the few times she did she got a woman from the phone company. They were having it out when the woman said to Trina, "You should be ashamed of yourself. Not so much for what you owe my company, but for how you treat your kid."

"What do you know?" Trina said.

"I know Travis has nothing to eat. That he's surviving on ketchup packets and what the people in your building are feeding him. I know he's out roaming the neighbourhood at all hours of the night."

"How do you know that?"

"I've been calling. He's been answering the phone. We've talked. Oh, he told me about his birthday. How you went out to get him a Happy Meal and didn't come home for two days."

"Well he's a kid. He exaggerates. He makes shit up."

"I know your type. Either you lie because you drink or it's the other way around."

"Fuck you. How'd you like me to barge into your home and talk to your kids? I bet they'd say some nasty shit about you."

"They'd tell you I'm not perfect but there's always food in the cupboards and I know where they are at all times. What's in your cupboards? Where's your kid right now?"

"In his room."

"Put him on the phone."

"I don't like him talking to self-righteous bitches."

Trina hung up. She checked Travis's room. Empty. Everything the woman from the phone company said, from what Trina could remember, was true. And though she would be ashamed of it later on, having some bitch from the phone company confront her over how she treated her kid wasn't enough of a jolt to get her sober. It got a few tears out of her, but that was all. The jolt came a month down the road, long after her phone got disconnected, when the cable went. She loved her soaps, and as pathetic as she knew it was, not knowing if Jay came out of his coma in time to stop Brooke from marrying Tad, the guy who poisoned him, putting him in the coma in the first place, was what sobered her enough to discover the eviction notice that had been slid under her door. That there wasn't any food in the apartment, she couldn't remember the last time she had bought groceries, and that her kid, just as the woman said, had been surviving on ketchup (empty packets littered the apartment) and what scraps the neighbours gave him (unwashed dishes that didn't belong to them were piled on tables and countertops and on the floor next to his bed). Ten years old and he was living like a stray dog. She realized she was worse than the crab-infested slut she'd been cursing the past several months. The slut only preyed on a horny man who should've known better. Trina had neglected her own kid.

It was a struggle but she was able to string enough sober days together to find another job waitressing. But one job was barely enough to keep them afloat, let alone pay the backlog of rent. She started checking the classifieds. She was looking for something she could do on the side, from home, like sell stuff over the phone—only she didn't have her phone back yet, but that was the sort of opportunity she was looking for. That was when she came across the ad:

NUDE MODELS WANTED
FOR ADULT MAGAZINES
FEMALE 18+ $$$
789-6743

The first time she saw it she didn't consider it. The next time, being a little more desperate, she tried to wonder what it would be like to have truckers in places like Texas beating off to her picture in small sweaty beds at the back of their cabs. The third time she walked to a nearby phone booth.

There was no answer. She hung up as soon as the answering machine came on. She went back later and called, and the second time she left the number at the booth. It smelled like an outhouse so she waited next to the booth in the empty parking lot of a closed down Chinese food restaurant. The Magic Wok had once had the best egg rolls in town. Its big yellow sign was like a fire in the sky. The place was always full. So was its aquarium of exotic fish whose names reminded her of the Hawaiian Islands. One day the restaurant didn't open. The story goes it got shut down by the Health Board: there were more rats in the kitchen than chicken balls.

In a way the Magic Wok reminded Trina of her marriage, only it was infested with crabs and when she confronted her husband all he had to say for himself was, "Quit your whining. I'm the one in jail for fuck sakes. Besides, compared to anything else out there, crabs are a walk in the park."

She held back her tears. Through the cage that separated them she called him a selfish prick.

"With the family I got, it's easy to be selfish," he said.

"What's that supposed to mean?" she said. "What?"

"Put it this way, I'd rather be here than out there with the two of you."

"You don't mean that."

"Of course I mean it. The kid, I don't even know where to begin. And you, you just put up with his shit, pretending that he ain't all that fucked in the head. But it's the two of you. You're both fucked as far as I'm concerned."

"I'll change. He'll change. You'll see when you get out."

"Fuck that…"

She was now shaking like a stroke victim, struggling not to cry.

"…fuck the two of you," he said, his face like a sledgehammer. Dark, wide and blunt. And as she crumbled he got up from his chair and banged on the metal door. It buzzed and he was gone.

Her eyes might have been on the Magic Wok but her mind was on the man she still loved when the phone rang. Instant dread, as if answering the phone was illegal. It took her a few seconds to find her voice.

"Hello," she said.

"You left a message," he said.

"I called about your ad."

"Sure. Have you ever done this sort of thing?"

"No."

"What makes you think it's for you?"

"I don't think it's for me. I need money, and quick."

"To the point, I like it."

"What are you paying?"

"That depends. What size are your tits?"

It caught her off guard, his question and the way he asked it, as casually as she'd ask somebody if they wanted gravy on their fries.

"Well?" he said.

"D," she said.

"Not bad, are you fat?"

"I'm not a rake."

"So you're chubby?"

"Not even."

"Blond?"

"Yeah."

"Everywhere?"

"Well, no."

He laughed.

"Very few of you are," he said.

She could feel herself getting angry. He had a way of making her feel cheap and insignificant like a set of tea towels from a dollar store and she would've already told him where to go and what she thought of him if she didn't need the money so badly. Again she asked what he was paying.

"I told you, that depends," he said. "If you're a mutt, you'd be lucky if I bought you a box of Milk-Bones. If you got the total package, face, tits, ass, everything, we could be talking 500 bucks for an afternoon's work."

"Christ."

"You don't think that's enough?"

"It doesn't matter what I think. I could use 500 bucks. Where do we go from here?"

He told her he needed to see her in the flesh before he could commit to anything. They made plans to meet the following afternoon at his place.

She showered, shaved everywhere, even painted her nails. The only polish she had was the colour of unripe peaches from a wedding she was in so long ago that the couple already had two kids and got divorced. The dress she wore was a relic from that same wedding. It was long and a little too tight in the chest and paunch but it matched her nails. She knew she was no Julia Roberts, but she felt good, the best she had in months. Still she was a bit anxious during the cab ride. It was over the money and not about what she was about to do. She was never the type to shy away from showing skin. When she was young her mom would dress her in the mornings but by lunch she'd have wriggled out of her clothes and be playing in the buff. In junior high she would show groups of boys her chest behind the school. It was her idea. She even let a few of the boys feel them. The bad ones. In high school she couldn't keep her clothes on either, though that was for a different reason.

When the cab pulled up to the house she was surprised. She didn't know what she had been expecting, but it wasn't a white bungalow with black curtains pulled shut and rose bushes that reminded her of her moms.

She knocked on the door. The sweet smell of the roses turned her stomach. If her mom was alive she knew she wouldn't approve of what she was about to do, but Trina hoped that on some level her mom would've been able to appreciate that, for the first time in her daughter's life, she was prepared to put her kid's needs ahead of her own.

The man was just as much a surprise as his house. He was younger than she expected. His hair was bleached and his shirt two sizes too small. He had all the makings of a soap star except that he had what looked like a large birthmark on his cheek. It was the colour of an old bruise and had the accidental look of something spilled. She wasn't sure where she knew him from but he was familiar and she figured he was a regular at one of the many restaurants she had worked throughout her career.

He gave her the once over. His eyes went back down her legs and he asked to see her ass.

"Out here on the step?" she said.

"It's dark in here," he said.

"So turn on a light."

"Consider this the first part of your audition. You pass, I let you in."

She sighed but it wasn't like she had much of a choice.

"Happy?" she said.

"Not exactly," he said, looking unimpressed.

She thought she knew what was coming next. She had a twenty in her purse and was already planning on paying a visit to the liquor store.

"I bought you Milk-Bones for nothing," he said.

She smiled, relieved. She was sure she didn't like him but at least he was easy on the eyes and funny in an old pervert sort of way. On top of that, and she knew this didn't say much about the company she had been keeping as of late, the Milk-Bone comment was the sweetest thing anybody had said to her in a long time.

It wasn't like he ever got out a calculator and did the math, these numbers were off the top of his head. Fifty percent of women who responded to his ad were real heifers, the type that spend their days grazing on sugar and anything deep-fried. So unless he knew of a magazine doing a special *Lovin' Large* issue, the only use he had for these women were blow jobs in the dark. Out of the other fifty, forty-five percent of the women were either old or ugly. They couldn't suck like the heifers, but their asses were small enough that he could bring himself to screw them from behind. Slap slap win win. The remaining five percent were hot, though most of them still had their shortcomings: saggy eyes, bad teeth, no chest or ass or cellulite like the clouds, varicose veins like angry forks of blue lightning. But then this woman standing on his step, she wasn't like any of them. She had the face, the body, but she was so much more than that. She was a blond beauty with an edge: the type to not wear panties on a first date; who men dream of dating at least once in their lives; who men want to picture when they masturbate; and the very girl that starred in most of his fantasies throughout high school and as recently as last month. He had her to thank for his only fetish.

"Come in," he said, holding open the door. As she brushed past him he got a whiff of hairspray and cigarettes and he was about to say something snarky, "Lucky for you nudie magazines aren't scratch and sniff," when he caught himself. He might have said that to one of the heifers, because chances are they would still end up giving him their best blow job in hopes he'd see the beauty hiding behind all that flab, but not with Trina. She had too much potential (her ass cheeks were like raw scallops, firm but fleshy, salt white) and they had too much history (at least in his mind they did, he still wasn't sure if she remembered him) to risk offending her.

"So, what?" she said.

"I want you to show me what else is under that dress," he said. "First things first, what do you drink?"

She was going to be good, say Pepsi, but she got to thinking: today isn't about behaving, lessons learned. It was about her kid, their future, getting paid, getting through the day the only way she knew how and then tomorrow she could begin sorting out the mess. That's what she had been doing the last fifteen years. What's one more day?

"Rye and seven," she said.

"I'll have one myself," he said.

"And I want to taste the rye."

"You will."

She was surprised at just how dark his place was. Heavy black curtains covered all the windows and by the light that crept through the sides she saw a place so tidy and void of clutter it didn't look lived in. More funeral parlour than home. The kitchen opened up into the living room and it took her a few seconds to realize that the moaning was coming from the TV. From what she could tell they were taking their time, going deep. That was how her husband fucked. It drove her near crazy, in a good way, but by the end of it she'd be begging for him to go harder. And he would, eventually. Only as soon as he felt she had given up on cumming would he go hard and try to fill her. He admitted this once when they were high or drunk or both, she couldn't remember which.

There were days when she missed having him around. His musk on the bed sheets. Feeling small in his arms. His truck idling out front of her work after a long shift. But there were days where she'd be so angry that all she could do to make herself feel better was to imagine him getting dragged into a cell, held down by a group of men and each one having a go and it being his turn to beg and plead. Last night, she imagined she had mailed him a certain magazine. Him flipping through the pages, getting hard, thinking all was forgiven until he came across her spread. What should have been for his eyes only could now be purchased for $4.95 at most convenience stores.

"Is your man all right with this?" he said, pouring rye.

"What makes you think I got one?" she said.

"Have a look in the mirror."

"Please."

"So?"

She took her drink without answering. The living room was more of the same thick black curtains and on the TV a maid or businesswoman or secretary was pinned between a mattress and a man, her stockinged feet were wobbling in the air as their moans now became grunts.

He sat on the couch and she went to the chair. She brought the cold glass to her lips, her eyes on the TV.

"Tasty?" he said.

For some reason she thought he was talking about the porn. The woman had pushed the man off and with his dick glistening from being inside of her gave it a suck before offering him her ass.

"What?" she said.

"Tasty enough for you?" he said, nodding at his drink.

"Sure," she said. She lifted her glass, alcohol spilling down her throat and she already felt less like herself, more in control.

"Are you into porn?"

"What do you mean by into?" she asked, glancing again at the TV as if it were an accident on the side of the highway. She was more curious than anything.

"I mean, do you like watching it?" he said.

"Depends if I like who I'm with," she said.

She thought she saw him smile.

"Porn is a dirty word," he said. "I don't get it. A dirty word for something most people like to watch. At least until they cum and the hangover sets in. They'll swear it off just like booze. They'll tell themselves they don't need it. That they're better than that. Some will even make promises to God. But there's always a next time. In case you're wondering, I'm not like most people," he said. "I'd watch porn with the pope and enjoy it. For me it's not just about jerking off."

"It took you a long time to answer the door," she said.

"Today wasn't one of those times. At least I washed my hands."

"Too bad."

"I like how your mind works. Dirty, like a man's."

"You aren't the first one to tell me that."

"I think of you in cowboy boots when I masturbate. Am I the first one to tell you that?"

It wasn't so much what he said but how he said it, as tender as a wedding vow.

"As great as a conversation as this has been, I really just want to get this over with," she said.

"Fine by me."

"So what do I have to do?"

"Take everything off."

"We didn't even agree on money yet."

"You're still auditioning. First I see everything you got. Then we talk money."

"At least turn that off."

"But we're coming to the best part. The maid--"

"Please."

As he searched for the remote she finished her rye in one gulp. Suddenly she was light-headed. Hot. All she could hear was her heart pumping blood in her chest and it was a lot like how she felt just before her first time. She was seventeen. Tony was three years older than her and he didn't believe that she was a virgin. She had a reputation. He soon learned that though girls lie, hymens don't. He ripped her open. She bled, it burned, but she loved him so much that when he came she cried she was so happy. She only ever wanted him. And even as he got more involved with stolen cars and there were rumours of other women she thought they would make it.

Just like her mom, who put up with her dad's moonshine years. He was grateful the rest of his life. And when the glaucoma took her mom's vision her dad taught himself how to cook. He'd also bring her for long country drives. Her mom said her dad would describe the colours of the sky, the types of wildflowers growing in the ditches. Trina always imagined Tony doing something like that for her. Them having their own little fairytale ending. Instead he gave her crabs.

"Whenever you're ready," he said.

She could barely hear him above her heartbeat. She could feel sweat on her forehead. She wanted another rye but couldn't bare the thought of delaying the inevitable. She struggled with the cheap zipper on the back of her dress before asking him for help. He smelled of perfume or cologne, she couldn't decide which. His warm breath on her neck gave her a chill. Her dress fell to the floor.

He clicked on a lamp. The light startled her. So did his birthmark. She had forgotten about it. But then maybe that was the point, she thought. Or maybe it was so that he could forget. Whatever the reason, she found it sad, the thought of a grown man hiding out in the dark.

"Does that say what I think it says?" he asked

She nodded. It circled her belly button, a red rose at the top and then in black ink, each letter the size of a thumb, *Tony's Girl.*

"Husband?"

"Yeah."

"Was it his idea?"

"What do you think?" she asked, not wanting buddy to know that it was her idea. She got the tattoo the day before the wedding. Tony was supposed to get one with her name too, but as the artist was doing hers he backed out. He wouldn't even tell her why, just a firm no, almost as if he had just realized that tattoos were forever.

"You should have told me about that," he said. "Magazines don't buy pictures of women who are branded."

"What do you mean?" she said.

"For most men it kills the fantasy. You'll always be Tony's."

His words were like a cold knife slicing through her.

"Look at it this way," he said. "its only skin deep."

"The same as your face," she said.

He walked into the kitchen. She saw the freezer door open. She heard ice cracking as he twisted the tray. She wasn't going to be able to come up with a damage deposit for a new place, let alone three months worth of rent money. So it was just a matter of time before she'd be back living with her dad, still working a nowhere job and struggling with booze and her kid and the break-up of her marriage. Her fairytale ending.

By the time he came back with two more drinks her dress was only half-zipped but she was ready to go.

She said, "Look, I shouldn't have …"

"And I shouldn't have," he said. "Now that that's out of the way I say we have another drink, get to know each other."

She hesitated, feeling split open, exposed, but really there wasn't much to consider.

He went through his share of women. Most of them were there and gone in what felt like minutes and he preferred it that way, quick and distant like a drive through. But with her he wanted it to be different. Personal. And as soon as he saw her tattoo he knew that that was his out (she'd never have to know that with the right light and angles he would've been able to hide it). But she wasn't plastic enough for the quality magazines and way too good for the low-budget fetish ones, so in a way he felt he was doing her a favour. He thought he might even help her out with money, depending on how they got along.

Waiting for her to say whether she would stay for another drink he wondered if she remembered him.

"You know who I am, right?" he said.

"You look familiar."

"It's Jody. We went to high school together."

"Sorry."

"They called me Wino."

"Wino," she said, and he knew by her tone she had forgotten him, which was worse than never having known him at all.

It seemed neither of them knew what to say next.

She finally took the drink he had offered her.

It was his turn to feel insecure.

"Mind if I turn off the light," he asked.

"I was hoping you would."

5

Most boys have stuffed teddy bears, guns, plastic toys whose purpose is to fight crime and wars and eliminate evil from the world. Jody never had toys like that. He had tools. One of the first tools his dad gave him was a flimsy metal plumber's wrench. The type that's disposable, that has a wide stubby handle and comes in the same box as a new faucet. His dad put it in his hand, probably drug him into the bathroom and set him up next to the toilet like he would a plunger and then told his wife to take the picture. In bright bathroom light, wearing blue overalls, a young Jody barely held on to the wrench. There was a confused look on his face. The tool was a mystery. At that age so was the toilet.

Jody did not remember the picture being taken, and only discovered it when he was fifteen. He was grabbing lunch money from his dad's wallet when he noticed the faded edge of a picture sticking out from all the business cards his dad collected. In the picture he looked like the world's youngest plumber about to work on the world's pinkest toilet, but that was not what struck him. It was the angle and the shadows, or how the light missed his skin in such a way that he could not see the large port-wine stain that had marred his face since birth.

The boys at school, at least the loud popular ones, called him Ketchup Face in elementary, which was shortened to Ketchup in junior high, and then replaced by Wino in high school. The girls, who were fortunate enough to be able to use make-up to cover their own blemishes, were too self-conscious to see beyond the mark. They were polite enough when he tried to engage them in conversation, but that changed when he asked them out or tried to get close to them at a school dance. Of course he dreamt about having surgery to remove it—if it wasn't for this fear that the scar would be worse than the actual birthmark. Of course he imagined his life without the mark—the boys would call him by the name his parents gave him, the girls would be willing to cozy up to him at a school dance and then make out afterwards in the back seat of his parent's car. When he found that picture in his dad's wallet it allowed him to feel, for as long as he stared at it, that a normal life was possible.

Leading up to his sixteenth birthday, Jody asked his parents for a 35mm camera so he could learn to create the sort of shadows he dreamt of hiding behind. Instead his dad gave him a soldering iron.

"You seem disappointed," his mom whispered, his dad on the phone talking to one of his foremen.

"I wanted a camera," Jody said.

"Every plumber needs a soldering iron."

"I'm not a plumber. I'm seventeen."

"You'll be a plumber soon enough. Besides, tools are expensive. One day you'll thank us."

Jody's parents never asked him what he wanted to do when he grew up. It was assumed, from an early age, that after finishing school he would go into the family business. His dad owned and operated the largest plumbing outfit on PEI, and had several crews that simultaneously worked on schools, hospitals, and government buildings. His dad had a passion for plumbing coupled with a way of making customers feel that they mattered. He never forgot a name thanks to a mnemonic system where Charlie Hanson got deposited in his memory bank as Handsome Charlie. He asked open-ended questions and listened to whatever was said, no matter how irrelevant, for however long it took customers to feel heard. He developed a unique greeting where he would shake customer's hands while patting them on the back as if he was trying to burp them. His dad credited the success of his business to hard work and a certain book he kept on his bedside table, which taught him ways of getting rich in business by developing deep interpersonal relationships. Jody received a copy of the book for an occasion he couldn't remember, and though he had only read the table of contents he wished he hadn't opened the thing at all, as it reduced his dad's success to a series of corny chapter headings, like: *The Handshake: Making it Memorable* or *Sally Fields or a Field of Sallys?*

On Saturday mornings, Jody worked for his dad, if you could call it that. He would climb into his dad's van and they would visit job sites. His dad would explain the purpose of the job, the budget, the schedule, the size of the crew, and if he was feeling inspired he'd even crack out his tool belt and perform some basic plumbing as if he was showing off his slap shot or golf swing. Then they would go for lunch, always a steak sandwich and bread pudding at the same diner where one of two waitresses brought their food and drink before they ever had a chance to order.

Jody was quiet on those Saturday mornings. His dad never stopped talking, even when he chewed his steak, as if he was afraid of what his son might say if given enough of a silence. When they were done eating his dad would take two twenties from his wallet and hand one to the waitress, the other to Jody. It may not be glamorous, he would say, but it's a decent, honest living. It leaves the world a better place.

Jody felt his dad was a good man who got most people, just not his son. At sixteen, at twenty-six even, decent and honest were two traits that didn't appeal to him. To be decent was to be forgettable, and girls already had enough of a reason to ignore him. And he felt that honesty was overrated, as harsh and unforgiving as florescent light.

Jody only had two friends. Tyler was poor, shy and had been growing the same wispy moustache since he was thirteen. Jimmy was one-half aboriginal, not that he advertised it, not that it made much of a difference since his dark oily hair and bronze pockmarked skin betrayed his heritage. He didn't live on the reserve, but he had relatives who did. With the money Jody had been "earning" each week, the money he had begun to save for the camera he never got for his birthday, Wino, White Trash and the Squaw (that was what the boys at school called them) drove out to the reserve and bought Ziploc bags full of contraband cigarettes from a cousin of Jimmy's. All Jimmy asked was that Jody kept his supplier a secret, and slipped him a few bucks. There was no worry about Tyler talking, and Jody made sure that his poor friend always had something to eat when his mom blotted her way to broke at bingo sometimes the same night she received her welfare cheque.

Jody began his senior year by selling two cigarettes for a quarter from his kitbag. His markup was minimal. It was never about the money, though on a good week he was able to triple his dad's twenty-dollar investment, but about getting noticed for a reason other than being another one of God's gaffes disguised as a test of character. He still got called Wino, by more people now than just the loud popular kids, but it no longer bothered him because it was said differently, not as insult but with respect, as if the name had been earned on the high school party circuit by always getting wildly drunk on cheap red wine and then finishing off the night by using the large tinted bottle for tokes.

"Wino," she said. Her brown bangs blew in the wind, so did her scent. She smelled of smoky green apples. Her cheeks were flushed and she wore fuchsia lipstick. Her dark eyes looked wet, like she had been crying, but then that could've been the wind.

"Hey," he said, wanting to sound casual.

"I love that name," she said.

"Thanks," he said, shuffling his feet so that she was not looking directly into the stain that he treated as a solar eclipse, afraid that it could singe retinas.

"It's funny, but cool."

"It's not my real name."

"I know," she said, trying to tuck her bangs behind her ear. Her fingernails matched her lipstick. She wore a boy's baggy jean jacket over a loose black dress that she held tight to her side so that it wouldn't fly up like her bangs. She wore dull brown cowboy boots whose heels were coated in dried mud from walking, he guessed, down a long country lane to catch the bus. She was Jody's age, but got around with boys who, in terms of high-school years, were much older.

"Look, will you sell me eight cigarettes and I'll pay you tomorrow?" she said.

He didn't want to sound desperate, but he wanted to leave an impression.

"I don't want to sell them," he said. "I want you to have them."

"And what do you want from me?" she said.

He glanced down at her boots. He already had an erection. "Nothing," he said. "You're nice. You like my nickname."

As soon as he said it he knew just how desperate he sounded.

"I won't be giving you a blow job."

"I know."

"But you've heard the rumour?"

"Yeah, but that's not why I want to give you the cigarettes."

"His ex-bitch started it. What do I care? I have him."

But he could tell she cared. He never had to worry about rumours because the cruel things people said about him were usually true. Still, he didn't consider their situations all that different.

"We're only here for another year," he said. "We'll grow up. We'll move on."

His mom said something similar after he came home from school sobbing so hard he began choking on phlegm. It wasn't that they would call him Ketchup, it wasn't that they would show off in front of pretty girls by surrounding him and using him as a pinball, it was how they would ignore him when they weren't abusing him, as if he were a cobweb in the rafters of their basements or a pebble in the treads of their shoes. He knew just how pathetic that sounded, he preferred torment to indifference, so he blamed his tears on Ketchup and pinball, and his mom offered him advice that he was quick to regurgitate, but still did not wholly believe.

"How about them cigarettes?" she said.

That was the only time he talked to her during their high school careers. Not long after that he heard another rumour. She was pregnant, the dad a dropout who still spent his days hanging out in trucks and cars in the school parking lot. She did look puffier, and it was winter and for a month she had worn the same two baggy dresses with bare legs and cowboy boots. The rumour was confirmed, at least in Jody's mind, when she dropped out of school.

Jody sold cigarettes all through his senior year.

Prom night was profitable. He skipped the actual dance, he knew enough to avoid the embarrassment of trying but failing to find a date, and at the after party in a remote field where clusters of cars blared music so loud the ground around them trembled like a flimsy plywood dance floor, kids got drunk and high as Jody sold them cigarettes. He sold out just after midnight, and then joined Jimmy and Tyler who were already wasted, sitting on the hood of Jimmy's graduation present that was parked far enough away to not be a part of any one cluster. Jody unscrewed a bottle of cheap red wine. He thought people would notice what Wino was drinking and get a kick out of it, but once the cigarettes were gone hardly anybody paid him any attention.

At least Jimmy and Tyler were drunk enough to believe they were part of the party and not outsiders looking in. They were talking amongst themselves, trying to embellish the events of their uneventful high school careers when a girl Jody didn't recognize came up to him, hoping he had saved a few cigarettes for himself that he would share with her. She held her hand over one half of her mouth and he figured she was chewing on her fingernails, nervous.

"Well, yeah," he said. He did have a few that he had saved for Jimmy and Tyler.

"Let's go smoke them," she said, leading him by the hand to a corner of the field where trees blocked out the light from the stars. Her hand was cold. He could hear the party as if it were a TV playing in his parent's bedroom.

"I don't really smoke," she said. "I tried it once, but I didn't like it. My name's Caroline. I go to Colonel Gray."

"Wino."

"Wino, I think you're beautiful."

She was still chewing on her fingernails. He knew she was hiding something. He looked to see if there were people behind the trees or crouched in the bushes, waiting to witness his vulnerability, the punchline to an elaborately cruel joke.

"It's dark," he said. "I'm sure you're drunk."

"So what if I am? I'm the same person, just braver."

"Wait till you see me in the light. Then we'll see how brave you are."

"You walked past our car. The headlights were on. You're beautiful."

He felt ugly most of his life and then a girl paid him the sort of compliment he thought he would only ever hear from his mom. A girl who seemed normal, who sounded sincere, and instead of embracing a beautiful moment in his life he said, "Prove it. I want you to prove it."

She leaned in, and at the last minute the cold wet nails that she had been chewing on slid across his cheek and through his hair. He shivered, nobody every having touched him like that before. He could taste the alcohol on her breath. This was his first kiss and it started out all lips, but gradually his tongue gained the confidence to explore her mouth. At one point the tip of his tongue slid over her upper lip, and he felt something, a crooked canyon in her flesh.

He instantly knew what she had been hiding with her hand. Why she thought he was so beautiful. How they could never be together outside of this dark field because when people saw them together they would think, good for them, that they found each other.

He took charge. He treated her as if she were a timed test whose result could help him salvage his high school career. In the minutes he had to finish he invaded a wire bra, cupped breasts, tweaked nipples, cut through pubic hair, slid a finger up a vagina, led a hand down his pants before guiding her head down in hopes that her mouth would coordinate efforts with her hand.

And she did. It seemed to him she took everything she knew about eating Freezies and applied it to blowjobs. She was mechanical in how she squeezed, pulled and sucked his dick. She repeated that until she was out of breath, and then she took a break, wiping her chin as her hand took over. It didn't matter that she lacked stamina or spontaneity, he was so turned on by the fact that a girl, any girl, was willing to wrap her mouth around his dick that within minutes he was ready to cum. He briefly entertained the idea of warning her, but he could hear the distant party made up of boys who had ignored him and girls who had rejected him his whole life. Jody was becoming a bitter young man, and on prom night the sweet girl with the cleft palate choked on a mouthful of his bitter as he imagined it was the dropout in a loose dress and cowboy boots kneeling in front of him. Rumour was she was no different than a prostitute, and would trade blow jobs for booze, drives home, those famous cowboys boots that found there way into almost all of his fantasies.

The summer after graduating from high school Jody began working full time for his dad. It wasn't like the other summers and Saturdays: no coffee and supply runs, no standing over grimy grunting plumbers, no pretending to listen to his dad while he dreamed up new, alternate lives for himself. This summer he was the one down on the floor grunting. He knew enough about plumbing to install valves, elbow joints, sinks, taps and toilets. And there seemed to always be enough work that he barely had time to eat whatever his mom had packed in his lunch, usually a tuna salad sandwich on soggy white bread. At the end of the day, having spent the last ten hours jammed up inside the bowels of some building or house, grimy from mystery liquids, stiff from all his contorting, his dad would come by the job site, inspect the day's progress, and drive him home. His dad would talk about the jobs they had coming down the pipe, a wrench in a plan that would end up costing them. Always the same two terrible puns, always more monotonous work, always they or them and Jody was afraid his dad was about to announce a name change. Doyle and Son Plumbing. The decals, the business cards, the ad in the phone book. Not quite as permanent as a birthmark, but close.

Supper would be ready as soon as they got home, though Jody stopped eating at the table with his parents. Plumbers were a grimy, homely lot and since there was nothing he could do about his homeliness he would focus his efforts on washing away any trace of the day. He would spend fifteen minutes in the shower, which included creating a thick lather of orange-scented mechanic's soap and then scrubbing his hands with a hard bristled toothbrush, and another five applying cream and coordinating his outfit. Jody's post-work cleanse was as much mental as physical, and once clean he would grab the mound of food his mom had plated for him and fall into the sofa in front of the TV. He was the one who operated the remote and chose the shows. He controlled the level of light in the room, which meant he pulled the thick curtains shut and turned off all the lamps. After he finished eating he left his plate on the carpet and stretched out, unwilling to share the sofa. Jody didn't feel a bit bad about commandeering the living room, relegating his parents to their bedroom like they were teenagers huddled around a 13 inch TV. In a way he was daring his dad to say something, and in his head he had already prepared a list of all the damaging things he would say.

Fridays were the only nights that Jody's dad insisted he join them at the table for supper. This was non-negotiable, but Jody's cleanses timed perfectly with how long it took his dad to fry bologna. Fridays after work, for as long as he could remember, his dad would stop by Norman's, a Lebanese grocer who imported and sold exotic and specialty meats and buy a hunk of the sausage wrapped in what looked like pantyhose. The grocer would always ask after the family and throw in a small paper bag of Iranian dates. Jody's dad would then come home to steaming pots of vegetables surrounding a cast iron pan, already hot. He would roll up his sleeves, wash his hands, peal off the pantyhose, slice the meat, spread bacon fat so that it covered the belly of the pan and when it was spitting he would fry the meat in batches. This was a tradition that his grandfather had started. That was back when bologna was a luxury not every family could afford. But it wasn't so much about the kind of meat as savouring with his family something real at the end of a long week during which he drafted and interpreted tens of thousands of theoretical words on flimsy paper. Jody's grandfather sold insurance. For Jody's dad, tradition was a religion.

Jody now accompanied his dad on his trips to the Lebanese grocer. Every Friday his dad would act as if he was the world's foremost expert in bologna and talk of how the sausage wasn't what it used to be, at least the stuff made in North America, the stuff found at every corner grocer. He would talk at length about how they were trying to mask the flavour of cheap flaky meat with spices.

It was the final day of August and already it felt like fall.

"This stuff, it's far from cheap," his dad said as got back in the van.

Jody nodded wearily and could already smell the bologna through the brown paper bag.

"Norman imports it from Europe. From Bologna, of all places. It tastes just like how it did when I was your age. The Europeans, they value tradition over anything else. They know they'd be nothing without it."

Jody chewed a date as his dad talked and drove.

"You'll ruin your appetite," his dad said.

Jody rolled down the window and spit out the pit. He grabbed a handful of dates.

When they came through the door there were no steaming pots of vegetables, no hot cast iron fry pan to greet them. Jody's mom was standing next to the kitchen table. She was holding a sheet of stiff pale paper, creased twice. It looked like she was about to deliver a speech.

"How could you do this to us?" she said. "How could you?"

Jody thought she was talking to his dad. Apparently, his dad did as well. He was as pale as the paper she was holding, taking short shallow breaths and unable to rest his eyes on his wife or son. Jody would always wonder what went through his Dad's mind at that moment. An affair at a trade convention? Money to a member of the legislative assembly in exchange for that contract to plumb the new hospital? Whatever it was, the truth was potent enough to transform his dad: the same receding sandy hair, the same puffy round cheeks, the same clear green eyes the colour of old Coke bottles only they didn't add up to the same man. He looked as guilty as a mug shot.

Jody's mom didn't see it. It turned out her anger was directed at her son.

"Art school," she said. "And I suppose you just forgot to tell us?"

"I'm on the wait list," Jody said. "I don't see what's the big deal."

"It says here that you've been accepted," she said, slapping the paper for emphasis. "It starts Wednesday."

"Art school?" his dad asked.

"Yeah, in Nova Scotia," she said.

"What would he do at art school?" his dad asked.

"Photography. He wrote an essay about a picture you keep in your wallet. I guess it impressed J G Hodgson, whoever that is."

"What does he know about photography?"

"Nothing," Jody said. "Isn't that the point of school?"

"How do you plan on paying for art school?" his mom asked.

"I've got money."

"Not enough."

"What do you know?"

"I know school's expensive."

"Maybe I've been selling drugs."

"You're a good boy. I don't believe that."

"Believe it. Want to buy some magic mushrooms?"

"You're angry. It's like you want to hurt us. To get back at us for giving you more than we ever had when we were your age."

Jody was shaking now, his teeth chattering. He couldn't focus his mind, articulate how he felt, so he said nothing. As the years passed and he revised this moment in his mind he imagined himself saying, "You're right. I am angry. I am getting back at you for trying to decide how I should live my life. MY LIFE!"

"What about the business? About becoming a plumber?" his dad said. He had always been afraid of disappointing his dad. Now was no different. All he could manage to say was, as if they were sitting at the table and his dad was trying to pass him the ketchup, "No thanks."

A mug shot one minute, a snapshot of devastation the next.

His mom handed Jody the letter and hurried after his Dad who had gone back out the door. An engine started. He wanted to be sure they were gone before reading. The letter was formal. Facts and dates on letterhead but there was a handwritten note at the bottom. It read:

Dear Jody,

You should know it is quite remarkable that you received acceptance to our school without a portfolio. That speaks to the strength of your essay. It is amazing to think that something as simple as finding an old photograph of yourself in your dad's wallet had the potential to change your life. I have no doubt we will teach you to create the sort of shadows you dream of hiding behind. I hope we also teach you to embrace light.

Best wishes.
Dr. J G Hodgson

Alone in the kitchen, Jody realized just how hungry he was, just how much he had been looking forward to his Dad's bologna. He went through the ritual of heating the cast iron pan, slicing the meat, and frying it in bacon fat. The smell filled the kitchen. The fat crackled as it exploded. He wasn't sure how long to cook the meat and he only removed it from the pan when it was blackened like marshmallows cooked over an open flame. If he had owned a camera, he got it in his head that he would've taken a series of pictures. Bologna looking like a woman's calf wrapped in pantyhose. A wooden cutting board with slices of bologna slumped over one another like dead soldiers. Sizzling bologna caught in a downpour of fat. He would've called the series of pictures "Last Supper".

He ate at the table alone. The bologna didn't taste nearly as good as when his dad fried it, but that wasn't the point. He filled his belly and wondered if Jesus felt like crying during his Last Supper.

On a small island of eccentrically small-minded people, Jody stood out for a reason he would only wish on his worst enemies, mainly the worst of the loud popular kids who either tormented or completely ignored him, the same kids he drew secret satisfaction from the idea that he may have helped hook them on cigarettes that later in life would give them cancer and make them wish, at the worst of it, for an early death like he once did.

In order to succeed at art school you had to stand out, find your angle, and work your angle into your art so that it stood out at least as much as you did. Jody had no choice but to stand out, which meant he didn't have to try all that hard like so many of the others who resorted to modeling their image after celebrities like Henry Fonda, Jesus, or Sid and Nancy, who brought attention to their veganism by wearing shirts that reminded people Meat is Murder, who organized protests over corrupt dictatorships in small countries they'd never been to, whose locations they couldn't even pinpoint on a map. Among art school types Jody's face was a canvas that had been marked with a stark truth they were searching for in their own art, and rather than pity they respected him, some even envied his condition.

His angle was shadows. He would follow them like seniors follow the weather. He would sit in class and note how they took over corners, hiding spiders and their webs and their feasts of dead flies. He would walk through the streets at dusk and watch as the shadows took over, getting ready for night. If I didn't have day classes I'd live my life in shadows or under the cover of night, he said on more than one occasion. I'd be the phantom of NASCD, he said in reference to the famous musical he never saw and was only vaguely familiar with its premise. When he would talk people would now listen. A lifetime of hurt suddenly amounted to something. Within a month of arriving in Halifax he had a room in a basement apartment, a whole circle of friends who like him didn't have many friends in their previous lives, and had already lost his virginity several times with girls as vulnerable and self-conscious as he was.

The virgin shtick lasted a semester. After that he developed a reputation as a skilled lover, somebody who would welcome almost anybody into his bed. Girls would solicit him at school, on the street, or the repeat customers would knock on his window at all hours of the night. They got what they wanted. A warm body, a hard dick, discretion, a darkness so thick they could hide from themselves. He would explore their bodies as much as they would allow. In the beginning it was with his fingers, but gradually his tongue grew to be as bold as his fingers were. Several of them were game for getting photographed. No clothes, the prop that really excited him was a pair of women's cowboy boots he had bought at a vintage store and kept next to his bed. They were beat up, brown, and brought him back to the days when he got raging hard-ons in the school parking lot.

Some were weirded out by the boots. Others enjoyed the idea of them so much that they came back with their own props. Jody collected pictures like jocks do medals and trophies.

Standing out, finding his angle, those were the easy parts. Learning the art of photography was not so easy. It didn't help that Jody was more dedicated to his social life than his craft. He was competent with the camera, could apply the rule of thirds, set his depth of field, and light almost any subject so that early on it was obvious he could make a career out of taking mundane portraits of families huddled around fireplaces or trees wearing the same goofy smiles and sweaters. But when it came to breaking the rules of composition in favour of style, he had difficulty recreating with his eye and camera what he saw in his mind. His pictures were just decent; their focal point usually a shadow that was lacking in definition or short on mystery. At the end of his first year one of his professors took him aside, told him that if shadows were his specialty they needed to be more penetrating. More haunting.

"You're taking pictures with the eye of a tradesman, not an artist," she said.

As far as Jody knew his professor was unaware of his history with the trades. Though she went on to pay his work several compliments, and encouraged him to take lots of pictures over the summer, all he heard in his head was one word on a loop as he hurried through the conversation and found refuge in a nearby bathroom stall. To be a tradesman among artists was about the worst failure he could imagine. He blamed his dad. From an early age he was groomed to think like a tradesman, the old photo he had found in his dad's wallet was proof of that. He approached photography the same way as he did plumbing, focused on getting the job done, sticking to code. For artists, he had realized, the job was never done. And the only reason they learned rules, or a code, was so that they knew how and when to break them. Jody left the bathroom a changed man, though it took him almost a summer to realize it.

He got a job as a bartender in the city, which meant he didn't have to go home for the summer. He had only been home once since he went away for school. At Christmas. He was in no hurry to go back. For almost four months the only sun he saw was at dusk or dawn. He slept all day, sometimes with a stranger lying next to him. He didn't pick up his camera once. When his friends came back to the city for school, most of them complaining of small town summers or bragging about European adventures, they commented on how pale he looked.

"Aren't phantoms supposed to be pale?" he said.

The semester was a month old when they found out he was taking a year off school. He told them that he couldn't afford it. That his dad made too much money for him to get student loans, yet his dad refused to help with tuition. They had no reason to doubt what he told them.

Jody tended bar for years. He lost touch with his parents and took certain measures so that they would remain out of touch.

His friends stopped asking him when he was going back to school and he was able to stop lying about it. Most of them moved away after they graduated. They all tried to make a go of it as artists, and for most of them that didn't work out so that they had to go back to real school or get real jobs that didn't satisfy them but still allowed them to work on what really mattered during their spare time which seemed to dwindle with every passing year and new responsibility. Jody drew secret satisfaction from his friends' failures, which he knew was a sign of just how much of a failure he actually was.

A young woman he worked with, that he had slept with when she first started waitressing at the bar, whom he photographed wearing just cowboy boots, told him she wanted him to take more pictures of her. An uncle of a friend back in Toronto was in the business of selling those sorts of pictures. Jody refused, afraid of all that went with putting himself out there.

Another year passed as forgettable as a rainy Tuesday.

Another unmemorable night at the bar when he looked up from the drink he was mixing and saw a resemblance to his mother in an old face staring back at him. Lips moved, all he heard was the band but he recognized the shape of his name. Jody delivered the drink he had prepared, took another order, and in that way tried to pretend it was just another night. But his hands trembled. He knocked over a jug of Clamato juice and because he didn't mop it up right away he slipped on it, almost falling. He fixed a round of White Russians sans milk.

Every time he made a mistake he glanced over at his mom who was as thin as a clothesline, her skin beginning to sag. She held her purse with both hands just below the surface of the bar. It was punk night, and he was sure her neighbour with the yellow mohawk was the reason for her vigilance.

During a lull at the bar Jody got a waitress to cover his post, passed the bathrooms and pushed through the emergency exit. It led him into a back alley that smelled of souvlaki and salt water from the nearby harbour. It was cool and misty. He could still hear the music that was muffled by brick.

"Son," his mom said.

"Don't call me that," he said with his back to her, staring at the blinking yellow lights from the Greek restaurant at the end of the alley.

"I've been trying to find you for almost a year."

"Did you ever think I didn't want to be found?"

"I have something I need to tell you."

"Same here. It was my life. Not yours. Not his. Neither of you had the right to decide how I should live it."

"I know that now. We knew what it cost us."

"Cost you? It cost me art school. An education. I dropped out after my first year because a professor told me I had the eye of a tradesman."

"I'm sorry."

"Why? You got what you always wanted."

"We wanted what was best for you. Your dad had already built a successful business. We thought it would give you a head start."

"It set me back nine years and counting."

"There's something I need to tell you about your dad."

"Did he send you? Did he think there was a better chance I'd listen to you?"

"There's no easy way to tell you this."

"I don't have all night."

He heard her take a breath.

"Your dad is gone," she said.

The first thing that registered in his mind was that his parents had separated, and whatever the reason he saw it in his dad's face almost ten years ago.

"It was a brain aneurism. It happened at work."

"All he did was work," he barely heard himself say, overwhelmed by the feeling that he and his heartbeat had suddenly vacated his body, were now floating above it like a pair of balloons.

"Not the last few years," she said. "He stepped back from the business. We really lived. We traveled. We went to Italy. We made it to Bologna. We even visited the factory where Norman gets his bologna. The owner served us small coffees and hard biscuits. They weren't anything to put in a postcard. Your dad ended up telling him that in our country coffee lasts and biscuits are soft. We all laughed. After that we had a wonderful talk about how much the bologna meant to our families."

"I need to get back."

"Tradition was everything to your dad. He talked about you a lot, you know. Especially on that trip. He wished you were there with us. He kept saying how he wanted to share Italy with you."

The steel door only opened from the inside. Jody rejoined his body just as he began walking away from his mom towards the blinking yellow lights at the end of the alley.

He heard quick footsteps. She grabbed his arm.

"You want to seem indifferent."

"I wish I was indifferent."

"I noticed you aren't wearing a ring," she said. "Do you have a girlfriend?"

"Dozens. I have the dirty pictures to prove it."

"I know you're hurting. I raised you, remember."

"What do you want from me? Tears? A eulogy?"

"I want to be there for you as you grieve. I don't think you should be alone during a time like this."

"Just look at me. I'm always going to be alone. The best I can hope for is for women to let me fuck them in the dark."

He shrugged from her grip, resuming his walk up the alley. He didn't mean to sound so bitter, so tragically alone, but it was one thing to hide the truth from a friend and it was another to hide it from his mom. She may have betrayed him by siding with his dad when it came to art school, but he could still remember the time she mentioned she must have misplaced some of her makeup. He was thirteen. "I won't be missing it," she said. "It was high time I treated myself to new stuff."

"Jody," she called out.

It was just sinking in that he would never get a chance to confront his dad as he had imagined so many times in his head; he would never be able to accept his dad's apology once they calmed down after the confrontation that his mom would've broken up with dinner or dessert or the assignment of a chore; he would never be able to grow old alongside his dad, to laugh with him, to consider him more than just family, his oldest friend.

"The house is yours if you want it," she yelled.

He kept walking but his pace slowed.

"I moved out right after it happened," she yelled. "I couldn't stay there. I know he would want you to have it. For it to stay in the family."

Jody told himself he did it for his mom, to help her adjust to life as a widow. He told himself he did it for his dad, for the sake of tradition, the least he could do was maintain the suburban homestead considering he had turned his back on the business. He even tried to tell himself he did it so that he would have something other than a box of nude pictures to show for his twenties, and so that he could have something to brag about when speaking with his artist friends who could barely afford their own houses, let alone dream of paying them off. The truth was, he moved home, back into his parents' old place because it was home.

6

Her mother would call them the nervous poos. She would say poo in a near whisper and afterwards would attempt to hide her smile with her bony blue-veined hand. Trina, however, in her deadpan called them the coffee shits because it would pour out of her like a steaming pot of fresh brew and there would be no giggling afterwards.

Trina had the coffee shits all afternoon. Her bowels would shake and gurgle like a cheap plastic percolator and then she would have to go. In the two hours it took her to do her hair and makeup she rushed to the toilet five times.

"You got fifteen minutes to get ready," she yelled. Her voice filled the small apartment and she realized she hadn't seen her son in hours. The ice in her glass was melting, watering down her rye. She went to see if he was in his room. Her hair was in curlers and she was wearing a tight black top and new nude pantyhose and a red skirt that had the same pattern as a bandana her ex used to wear. When she bought the skirt she'd had him in mind.

Her son's room was empty and she searched the rest of the apartment. She had been afraid something like this was going to happen. She could already see herself, hair in curlers and tramping down the road roaring her kid's name. Her neighbours at their windows, watching. No wonder she had the coffee shits. Then she went back to her room because she decided the least she could do before she went out looking was remove her curlers.

"Where have you been?" she said. Her son sat at the edge of her unmade bed. Cracks of light came through her blinds and he was flanked by an army of dust motes.

"Under your blanket," he said.

"Why?"

"I was watching you make yourself pretty but when you started putting those things in your hair I got bored and went to sleep."

She sat on the floor in front of the mirror. She inspected her face and said, "We're leaving in fifteen."

"I'm ready," he said.

She glanced at him through the mirror. His head was covered in wild cowlicks and by the creases on his cheek she could tell what side of his face he had been sleeping on. "At least wet your hair and comb it," she said.

"I don't like him," he said.

"You never met him," she said, carefully removing the curlers from their nests of hair as if they were delicate blue eggs.

"I never met the devil but I know I don't like him."

"He isn't the devil, I guarantee you that. He's been good to me at a time when I really needed it."

"But I've been good to you. I'm your man, remember?"

"Yeah, you're my man around here. You've been good to me in a different kind of way."

"How can I be good to you like he's good to you then?"

"You can't. We've been over this," she said, and she didn't mean to sound so abrupt but it was obvious he still didn't get it. Through the mirror she watched him think it through. His conclusion, at least for now until she said or did something that convinced him otherwise, left him looking as forlorn as a dog left locked in a car.

"And what did I tell you about his birthmark?" she said.

He thought about it. "You told me it looks like a bruise."

"That's because you asked me what it looked like. What else?"

He stayed quiet.

"I told you he's sensitive about it," she said. "So don't stare at it. No smart remarks. And if you behave, well, you know where I'll take you."

Still he was quiet. Travis was simple in some respects but could be shrewd when it came to getting his own way.

Her bowels shook and gurgled.

She had time to remove her curlers and briefly admire her hair. It dangled and shone like silk ribbon. She decided she would take the time and curl it more often. Then she rushed to the toilet.

On the cab ride across town Trina sat by herself in the backseat, the sun dropping, its light draining from the streets and lawns that were a mess of fallen leaves. Her son was trying to act like a man up in front, next to the cabbie, by talking about the car. She heard him say it sounded like a happy cat. Some man.

She was still not quite over her ex. Thoughts of him were what compelled her to drink whereas the anticipation of her time with Jody helped her to maintain her sobriety between dates. Except for today. She had showed up at the liquor store early this morning. When she tried the locked door two women inside, butch and bitter looking, looked up from their gossiping with faces that judged her in a glance. She served women like that every shift, the type who asked for an extra cup of coleslaw and then complained about how long it took to arrive. Rather than deal with their disapproving glances until the store opened she went for a walk through town.

At seventeen she would never have imagined her life would turn out this way. Separated, snared by a life she never chose, that was born from one bad decision after another. She decided she wasn't so much an alcoholic as she was addicted to forgetting. She wished her sister was alive so that she could've called her. She wished she would've just said yes when Jody asked her to move in. Instead she told him she wanted him to meet her son first. See how they got along. Then they could see about moving in together.

She watched the colour drain from his face when she told him this. She could tell he thought it was him. Everything that went wrong in his life, every bit of rejection, he seemed to trace back to the mark he was born with. What he didn't seem to get was that this had nothing to do with him, she was just trying to avoid more of those same bad decisions that had stalked her since she found out she was pregnant and dropped out of school in grade ten. A while ago she bought a book that was supposed to help her study for her GED. It had never been opened; all it had ever been used for was as a coaster. She tried to explain all of this to Jody, that for the past decade she had been buying lottery tickets, basically waiting for something or somebody to come along and change her life.

"I gotta be better," she said. "Make better decisions. It's time I took responsibility for the rest of our lives."

It was a nice speech but he only heard what he wanted to hear. Suddenly he was skeptical, already distancing himself, acting aloof like a sullen teenager.

"Move in or don't," he said, getting up off the couch. He walked over to the window and looked out. "I was just trying to do you and your kid a favour," he said. "Considering you're about to be evicted."

"Baby, I know. It's not you," she said, coming up behind him. She wrapped her arms around him. He was slim but defined. He smelled as seductive as a woman but he was all man. She unbuttoned his jeans.

"I know it will work out," she said. "I'll see if I can find my boots."

"Whatever," he said.

That was five days ago. Now she had the coffee shits because she knew, despite her repeated warnings and an attempt to bribe her son with the promise of a visit to McDonald's, he was going to say something to Jody about his birthmark. She knew Jody would overreact and she would be torn between wanting to comfort him and wanting to tell him to get over it. She wasn't sure when it happened but she no longer noticed his birthmark. It was as insignificant as a mole and she refused to let him hide in the dark, at least not when they were together.

Jody came to the door and before he even invited them inside his eyes followed her legs down to her boots. They lingered there. He seemed to forget who and where he was.

"Aren't you going to invite us inside?"

"Of course," he said. "Come in."

He stepped back from the door and they followed him into his kitchen. The lights were low, every switch in the house on a dimmer, but at least they were on.

"You must be Travis?" he said. "I'm Jody," and he stuck out his hand. Again he glanced down at her boots.

"Shake his hand," Trina said. "Men shake other men's hands. It's a sign of respect."

But Travis wouldn't lift his hand. He wouldn't even speak. All he did was look Jody in the face and she was afraid of what was going through his mind. Not that Jody noticed. Most of his attention was devoted to a pair of scuffed brown cowboy boots. They used to be loose on her calves. She wore them for much of grade ten, until they could no longer accommodate her swollen feet, which was around the same time she gave up trying to hide her growing belly.

Before Jody had asked her to move in with him he admitted her boots were one of the highlights of his high school career. The focus of many marathon masturbation sessions, which had resulted in his own collection of women's cowboy boots.

"For who?" she had said. "All your other women?"

"None of them even came close to looking as good as you did in yours," he said. "Besides, you should be flattered. You're the one who inspired it all."

And strangely, she was.

Jody pulled back his hand when Travis wouldn't shake it. "That's all right," he said. "We'll get to know each other first. Then we'll see about shaking hands."

She smiled and mouthed thank you. She hung her coat over a kitchen chair and went to take off her boots.

"Don't," he said, his tone a little too firm. "I want you to leave them on," he said, and just as she was struck by the feeling she really didn't know him at all he began to fix her a rye and seven. And she loved that, being taken care of for a change. He asked Travis if he could get him anything to drink.

"The least you can do is answer him," Trina said. "All this talk of being a man and you're behaving like a spoiled kid," she said, but her words didn't seem to register.

Travis was still standing just inside the door. His eyes hadn't left Jody's face since they arrived. His hands were tiny trembling fists.

"Why don't we go out to the living room?" Jody said.

Trina motioned to Travis to follow them. "Please," she said.

"You're wrong about his birthmark," Travis said.

"Don't," Trina managed to say.

"It doesn't look like a bruise," he said. "It's a Grimace."

They all went silent. Sweat had soaked through her shirt. Her bowels were simmering. A window must've been open and she could hear birds in the silence.

"Grimace, like from McDonald's?" he asked.

"Yeah," she said, embarrassed, looking down, then over at the open window where the field out back of his house was now enveloped by night.

"I've heard worse."

"I'm sorry," she said, and again she caught him staring down at her boots.

Startled, he looked up and said, "Let's go get comfortable. He can join us if he wants."

It would be a while before she would realize today had been marred by yet another bad decision. It wasn't following Jody and leaving her son to wait by the door—that was his choice. Her bad decision had been wearing those boots. They were all Jody seemed to notice, he didn't even comment on her curls, or her skirt that was so tight it cut into her like a dull knife when she sat down. And he barely noticed her son or seemed to consider what was said when his birthmark was compared to a cartoon monster designed to peddle fast food. They moved in together, and over time Trina realized that Jody would never be able to accept her son for who he was or forget what was said that first night. And her son, she realized, would always feel as if she had abandoned him for her boyfriend. But as hard as it was trying to play peacekeeper between the men in her life, she preferred that role to raising her son on her own.

7

It wasn't me, Travis, when I tiptoed into the kitchen, pushed my bum against the wall and opened my eyes wide and round like a fly.

"Mind if I finish that?" Jody said.

"My bacon?" Mum said.

"Yeah."

I knew Mum better than anybody, I'd lived with her my whole life, and one thing you didn't do was ask to eat her bacon. She didn't eat it very often, but when she did she cooked it crispy and ate it slow. She just loved the taste, so much that she sometimes ate it like hard candy, sucking it until every bit of flavour was gone and then chewing what was left.

"Finish it," she said. "I'm full."

I watched him take her bacon and I was shocked. She was a different person when he was around. A nicer person. She smiled more and with her painted face and curled hair she looked like one of those happy girls on the covers of magazines. And instead of spending all night in her green work uniform she wore pretty flowered dresses and old brown cowboy boots that used to live at the back of her closet. Jody was the one who bought Mum the dresses, and I soon figured out why. He liked how easy it was to reach up under them when he thought I wasn't watching. His hand would stay up there exploring and she would smile or shiver but what he didn't know was that I was always watching.

"I missed you, baby," she said.

"I missed you too," he said, chewing her bacon.

"I'm not the same person when you're gone. It's strange, I feel like the old me. I drink more."

"Huh."

"A lot more. If you went downstairs and counted the bottles, you wouldn't be happy with me."

"Are you saying that you were bad when I was gone?"

"Yeah."

"I don't like the sound of that."

"You'll just have to let me make it up to you then."

"And how will you do that?"

"I'm sure you have an idea."

"What about the kid?"

"I'll tell him that if he leaves us alone for our happy time, I'll bring him to McDonald's for his."

Jody smiled like he just heard a funny joke. He bit off a piece of bacon.

Mum went back to reading her flyers.

I smiled but only in my belly.

Since there was nothing going on at the table I looked out the window at the highway that went from one side of Canada to the other. When I was Travis I liked to lay by the highway with the bugs and empty chip bags and wonder what cars or trucks were on their way to Toronto. I liked Toronto even though I was never there because Miles told me it was so big you could wish for anything and find it around the next corner. That happened to him when he'd stopped there on a bus trip from Calgary to PEI. He told me his back was so sore from the ride that all he could think about was getting a rub. And just around the corner from the bus station was a flashing pink sign, Mama Jan's Massage. He went inside and a Chinese woman was sitting behind the counter smoking a brown cigarette. Miles told me that her eyebrows looked like they were painted on, like little brown frowns above blue eyelids. Her nails were white with tiny bouquets of black flowers. She was more paint than a Picasso, Miles said.

"How old?" she said.

"Eighteen," he said.

"Mama Jan old enough to be your grandmother. Joking. Mother. I'm old enough to be your mother," she said, not knowing that his mum had just died and he didn't like talking about her. "Deluxe or basic massage?" she said, and either she did pushups with her eyebrows or crunches with her forehead, Miles wasn't sure which.

"I've got thirty bucks," he said. "Whatever that will get me."

"I send you in room with girl, cost you over double thirty bucks. Massage with me, in closet, it cost you only thirty bucks. Basic but me good. Happy endings guaranteed."

She stubbed out her cigarette and led him into a room with towels, sheets, a mop and so much bleach that it smelled like a pool. The only place to sit was a seat from the back of a van. It was already reclined.

"Take off shirt and sit," she said.

She walked around him and ran her fingers through his hair. They were strong like a man's and smelled of cigars. They moved down to his shoulders and chest. When they pinched his nipples he realized what she meant by happy ending.

When he got back on the bus he slept all the way to New Brunswick and there wasn't much trip left after that.

I liked Miles' Toronto story. Someday I wanted one of my own with an ending as happy as his.

Mum finished with her flyers and said, "There's something I've been meaning to tell you. It has to do with Travis."

His mouth hung loose like a dog's as she told him about the cop knocking on our door.

"Jesus, Trina."

"He didn't do anything wrong. He was home all night with me."

"Likely."

"What's that supposed to mean?"

"You were drunk the whole time I was gone."

"I never said drunk."

"Where is he? Travis, get in here!"

"Look behind you."

"Travis, what happened with you and Ada?"

I tried not to blink. I even held my breath because I wanted him to forget I was there. That was what a good fly on the wall did.

"Travis, answer me," he said. "I know you can hear me."

"There's no use," she said. "Lately he's started going into these trances. It's like he's in a whole other world. He can't see us, he can't hear us. It's strange."

"Why's he standing like that?"

"Like I know."

"He's your son, you should."

Jody got out of his chair and came up to me. He looked into my eyes. I stared at the big Grimace-like birthmark on his face and I tried to hold in my smile because I was still thinking of what Mum said earlier about taking me to McDonald's.

"Sit back down," Mum said.

"He's smiling," he said. "Trance my ass."

"It doesn't matter. Sit. Please."

"It does matter. Ada was a sweet woman. She wouldn't hurt a fly."

That got another smile out of me.

"I know," Mum said.

"Why aren't you more upset?" Jody said.

"I was. I am, it's just, where are you going?"

"Out to the couch."

Before she followed him she bit into a piece of bacon, set it back down on his plate and then looked at me and went shush. The couch squeaked. I couldn't see them but I was still able to hear them like they were in the kitchen. It was smart of me to land on that wall.

"He scares me," Jody said.

"He shouldn't scare you," Mum said. "You just have to accept that you won't ever understand him."

"That's a terrible attitude to have."

"Nobody has ever understood him, not teachers, counselors, even me for Christ's sake. Whatever happened to Ada or the crow, we have to forget. It's like, I don't know, what's happening in Iraq. They can't always be afraid of going out in public because there's bombs falling. Scuds or whatever. There comes a point when they just need to accept that it's happening. Get out and get on with their lives. That's what I'm getting at. His dad could never do that."

"What about the crow?"

"What?"

"You didn't tell me anything about the crow."

"It's nothing. The last time I mowed the lawn I found a dead crow in the yard."

"How'd it die?"

"I don't know."

"You do. I can tell."

"It was like somebody had stepped on its head."

"By somebody you mean Travis?"

"He never did anything like this before."

"That doesn't mean it wasn't him."

"Baby, come on."

"Don't. I'm serious. Take your hands off. You're always trying to end fights that way."

"You never seemed to have a problem with it before."

"I do now."

They were quiet and though Mum didn't know it was me who crushed the crow's head I did warn her. I told her there were lots of crows breaking into brains lately and stealing secrets and I was going to do something about it. I guess she didn't warn Jody. Maybe she suspected he was keeping a lot of secrets and was hoping the crows would help uncover them.

"Anything else happen when I was gone?" he asked.

"Not really. No, no."

"I can tell you're lying. Out with it."

"When I was making his bed I found a few pictures under his pillow. I don't know where he found them but somebody might want to do a better job of hiding them."

"What did you do with them?"

"I took them," Mum said.

It was a lot of work being a fly on the wall, staying still and quiet for minutes and hours, but what I just learned made it all worthwhile. Those were my favourites of all of Jody's pictures and I thought they were gone. But now that I knew Mum took them I would only have to search her purse or her room and they would be mine again, only this time I would hide them in a better place.

The couch squeaked and Jody said, "Jesus."

"Kids get into things," Mum said. "It's nothing. Don't get so worked up."

"Why wouldn't I be worked up? I come home to you telling me that life with Travis is like being caught up in the Gulf War."

"Baby, that's not what I meant and you know it."

The phone rang.

"Don't answer it," said Mum.

"Hello," he said. "Hold on."

She talked into the phone and the floor creaked. Jody was back in the kitchen. He popped a piece of bacon in his mouth and came up close.

"I know you can hear me," he said. "I thought I could make this work. Me, her, you. I was wrong. I don't know what you had to do with Ada's death, but I'm going to make sure you get what you deserve."

I told him that this fly on the wall was going to make sure he got what he deserved. "Bzzzzzzzz," I said. "Bzz, bzz, bzzzzzzz."

"You little shit."

"Jody," she said.

"Trina," he said.

"Leave him alone" she said.

"I'll leave you both alone, if you aren't careful."

"Baby, don't say that," Mum said.

"I'll say what I want," Jody said. "I can handle you, it's him I don't know about."

He went down the stairs to the basement and Mum followed.

Jody maybe leaving us alone was even better news than finding out what happened to the missing pictures or hearing Mum tell Jody she was going to take me to McDonald's. I knew flies didn't smile but I couldn't hold it in.

I flew over to the table. Two strips of Mum's bacon were still on Jody's plate. I didn't think flies ate bacon either but I wanted to be not careful and I ate one of the strips. It tasted good but when I finished chewing I didn't feel satisfied. There was one piece left and before I ate it I broke off an end and put it in my pocket. For later, for Mum.

When Jody's plate was empty I went back to being me, Travis. This was the best fly on the wall I ever was but I knew I needed more practice. This was my third time being one since two weeks ago when I got the idea from the police officer. He came by the house in his uniform. I made him take off his boots because I couldn't have him bringing mud into the house like Miles did. He asked me more questions about the fire. I said me and Ada were having a good party until the fire crashed it. She got burned and I went home. He shook his head. He said, "If only I were a fly on the wall."

Mum came home from work just after that and told me that there was a loonie in her purse for me. She told me to walk to the store and get myself a treat. Usually I had to beg for loonies and if Ada had've got out of the house as quick as I did right then I bet she would've lived.

On my way to the store I thought about how I would like to be a fly on the wall too. But I didn't want to be the type of fly that got lonely and flew around heads, buzzing, until people were driven crazy and went and got the swatter off a nail in the closet. I wanted to be the type that could stay still and quiet for hours, that heard and saw everything, that people forgot about. That way I could learn secrets. And the secret I wanted to learn most in the world was what Jody did to make Mum happy again. Once I could make her happy like that without his help, I would take her by the hand and lead her down to the basement. I would lift the piece of board that looked like part of the wall. I would slide the box out and open it. She would see all the pictures of these girls. He was in some of them. So was his bird. And Mum would finally be mine again.

8

The day was grey and muggy. Trina was riding in a cab through town, smelling of onions and sweat and glad to be off work. One of the girls had called in sick. She had five too many tables. No matter how fast she moved the service was slow and the tips were lousy. Her thighs chafed. Now all she wanted was to lie in front of the TV with a cold drink and forget her shitty life for a while. There was no doubt in her mind that tomorrow and the days after were going to be a lot of the same. But then Jody would be home.

The cab turned onto her street. She was deciding between vodka or beer when she saw what was parked in the driveway.

"Christ," she said.

She paid the cab driver, leaving the sort of tip she would've liked herself. She hurried down the driveway and up the stairs. She opened the door and there was the same cop talking to her son.

"What's going on here?" she said.

The cop was a big man with a boyish face and he'd been there twice before, asking questions about the fire.

"I was just having a word with your kid," he said, and he looked her up and down, his eyes lingering on her chest but she was used to that. Men staring all hungry like she had two T-bones pinned to her chest.

"We already told you what we know," she said. "He was home all night with me."

"That's not what he just said."

"No?"

"No."

She looked over at Travis. His hair was uncombed and lunch was on his face and she was terrified of what he just told the cop. Could be nothing, could be enough of something that the cop was able to piece it all together. Her kid, the fire, Ada smoldering in the bushes.

"Mum is gonna have a few words with the cop," she said. "There's a loonie in my purse. I want you to take a walk to the store and buy whatever you want."

"I still have a few things I need to ask him," the cop said.

"You can ask me," she said. "He's done enough talking for one day."

Her kid was gone before she had her shoes off. Her feet felt bruised as she walked over to the cupboard and brought down the vodka. Yesterday's glass still sat on the counter. She didn't bother with ice or lime and went out to the living room and fell into the couch.

"Where are you going?" he called out.

"If we're gonna talk, I might as well be comfortable," she said, and by the time the cop entered the room the glass was half empty and her hair was down.

"I feel bad for you," he said. "I really do. But you gotta remember, a woman died in that fire."

"Like you need to remind me. Every time I look out the window is reminder enough."

The cop walked across the living room and pulled back the curtain.

"Sure," he said.

She didn't even have to look to know what he was seeing. The siding like a burnt marshmallow, gooey and black. There was plywood covering the picture window that Ada jumped through to escape. The glass sliced her throat and she was dead before she hit the ground. The cop told her that on his second visit. That and the fact that they were still trying to figure out if Travis had anything to do with starting the fire.

The cop let go of the curtain.

She thought about what she was going to say next, and as she was thinking she crossed her legs and his eyes followed them.

"He isn't right in the head," she said.

There was sweat leaking down his temples. His eyes wouldn't stay still. "You told me already," he said.

"I mean he really isn't right."

"I've seen the file," he said, grinning.

Since the cop was skeptical she decided to tell him the sort of everyday story that would never make its way into an official file but was more telling of what life was like with Travis than labels or medication.

"A couple years ago Travis wanted a cat," she said. "Every day he pestered me for one. He wouldn't shut up about it but I kept telling him no. The reason being we lived in an apartment and it didn't allow pets but try explaining that to him. So he kept asking and I kept refusing and then one day he just shut up about it. And I thought great, finally some peace. A bit of time passed before I noticed this smell. It was in our apartment but it was also in the halls. It wasn't too strong at first but it still got everybody's attention. I thought it was rotten potatoes, but as it got stronger an old man who lived in the building and fought in some war said that that was no potato. He said that that was the smell of rotting flesh. So the super had this exterminator come in, thinking it was a dead mouse or something, but when he searched the building he found nothing. And the smell got worse until it was in my clothes and skin and finally even food tasted all skanky and I got fed up. I searched the whole apartment. Just in case, you know. And you wanna know what I found in Travis' bed? A dead cat."

"Christ, and all the kid had to say for himself was that he wanted a cat, so when he found one on the side of the road he brought it home. Every night for nearly a month he slept with roadkill in his bed. And the strangest part of all of this was that when I wrapped it up in his sheets and threw it in the garbage, he cried like I had killed it or something."

The cop stared at her. She didn't think he knew what to say.

"When I said he isn't right in the head, I meant he really isn't right," she said.

"Sure, fine, I get it. Your kid's got issues. That doesn't change what happened."

"Like hell it doesn't. It changes everything. Cause there's only two people who know what happened. One of them isn't right and the other one is dead. So I don't know how somebody like you can think he's got it all figured out."

"Lady, there's no thinking about it. I know."

"You know what he told you. I'm sure that isn't much."

"It's enough."

"Yeah?"

"Yeah."

"What exactly do you know?"

"I know he didn't start the fire."

"So he did nothing wrong?"

"You wish it were that simple."

"What do you mean?"

"I know he was with her when the fire started. I know he watched her burn and did nothing to try and save her. Absolutely nothing. The worst of it was he left her burning and didn't tell anybody she was trapped in a fire. It may not be manslaughter, but it's something."

As awful as she felt about what happened to her neighbour, the way she saw it, all her son was guilty of was bad timing. And getting as far away as he could from fire, some would consider that good sense.

She glanced at the cop's hands. The gold band on his finger. She was afraid of what he meant by "something." Her kid never had a chance and she had her share of blame in that.

"What will it take to make this go away?" she said.

He said nothing.

"I mean, is there anything I can do? You know?"

His answer came in the form of a face so firm with disdain it reminded her of her dad's when she was young and she came home in the mornings still drunk, her eyes dark clumps of mascara and her pantyhose torn because when her ex wanted inside of her nothing got in his way, especially not pantyhose. One of those mornings, unknown to them all, Travis was already growing in her womb. Grade eleven and a kid on the way and her sister talking about taking her son and following her husband out west and her mom going blind and her dad so wrecked in the head and heart he didn't talk for a year. He spoke with just his face but still managed to say plenty.

"Don't look at me like that," she said to the cop.

"I'm married," he said. "I'll look at you any way I want."

"Don't think I don't notice your eyes. How you keep glancing down at my tits."

"Like hell I've been looking at your tits."

"Funny how the truth only matters when it's convenient for you."

"Don't talk to me about the truth. You've been lying to me all along, saying he was home with you the night of the fire."

"So he might've gone out. You said it yourself, it's not like he started the thing."

"You don't think he did anything wrong?"

"All I'm saying is that even if he did what you said, it's not the worst he could've done."

"I came here today feeling bad for you. But you know what? It's not you who I should've been feeling bad for. It's your kid. He's stuck with you."

The cop walked out to the kitchen.

She followed, found him tying his boots.

Her hands were unsteady but they managed to find the zipper at the back of her dress. Once they found the clasp of her bra she was just wearing just her panties and socks and didn't feel so sexy stinking of onions and sweat and feet but this wasn't about her.

Before he had a chance to speak she dropped to her knees and pushed her face into his groin. He grabbed her hair and pulled and she gritted her teeth but held onto his belt knowing she had everything to gain and he had everything to lose. He didn't have much fight in him. He wouldn't let go of her hair, though he stopped pulling and with her lips she could feel him growing through the polyester. She blew him in the kitchen before leading him into the bedroom.

They fucked. He was stiff at first, but then he got into it and before she knew it he was moaning and hugging her tight like she was his wife. She was bone dry and it burned but she didn't feel sorry for herself knowing it was a tickle compared to what Ada had endured. Eventually he let out a low groan, it sounded more like he was emptying his bowels than his testicles, and it was over. He was still panting when he rolled off of her and they lay on their backs on an unmade bed, her body damp with his sweat.

Eventually he said, "This never happened."

"It never happened," she said, staring up at the ceiling, his cum leaking out of her. "The same as your conversation with my kid today didn't happen."

He stayed quiet. She knew he was working it out in his head.

After a while he got up off the bed. He pulled up his pants and buckled his belt and before he turned to go he gave her the sort of look you'd give a mother who in her tired rage shook her screaming baby like a paint can. But all she did was try and protect her kid. All she did was try and save him.

The cop was soon gone and she got under the covers. She closed her eyes. She thought of things. She saw things, and one of the things she saw clearly in her mind was the cat in her kid's bed, intestines spilling out of its stomach and this yellow liquid leaking from its eyes so that it almost looked like it was crying at the disgrace of it all.

9

All families have their halcyon days. Days recalled so often and with such vigour and embellishment they form the lore that binds them through the generations, allowing them to survive the feuds, heartbreaks and fatalities that come with being a family.

Trina's family, as far as she was concerned, hadn't had a halcyon day in a long time. The last one happened several years ago and for all she knew it only survived in her memory because three of the six present were dead. This was a day she revisited often, sometimes when drunk, sometimes it was the reason she poured that first drink because she found it hard to bear the thought that there was no chance there would ever be a day like that again.

It was before the cancer, jail, booze, and Jody. It was back when she was still young enough to believe, like the ballads on the radio, that love may be a battlefield but it lifts you up where you belong.

That day began with the sun shining down through the small basement window onto the far wall of their bedroom. Her son must've come into their room in the night and was now sprawled at the foot of their bed like a dog. Her husband was lying next to her, heavy phlegmy breathing, radiating heat like a potbellied stove. Careful not to disturb either of them she sat up. Lit a cigarette. She always smoked the first of the day differently. She took her time with it, her mind meandering like the lazy blue smoke, still not quite awake. A few minutes to herself where she was neither wife nor mom, just a girl who grew up way too soon.

A knock on the door startled her. She looked at the alarm clock and her first thought was that something was wrong.

"Twenty six and sunny." Those were the first words out of her big sister's mouth. She lived in Calgary. She wasn't supposed to be home this summer, having recently left her husband and bought a new house. Yet there she was barefoot in cut-off jeans, a tank top, freckles up her arms and a fresh cluster of them on each cheek. Her fine red hair was windblown. Trina might've been the pretty one but she knew she would never be able to rival her sister's glow.

"When did you get home," Trina asked.

Her sister said late last night. Told her to get ready. That they would talk on the way out.

"Out?" Trina asked.

Her sister repeated the forecast. Told her they were spending the day at the beach. When Trina said that she was supposed to work her sister said that she was supposed to be in Calgary. Plans change.

Rolled down windows, bangs blowing, cheap corner store sunglasses, bare feet on the hot vinyl dash, the radio saying they had already surpassed the day's projected high, her son asleep in the backseat, never having really woken up, which told her he was up again most of the night. Tony had to work but said they may see him later on. Trina knew that meant they wouldn't be seeing him, that he'd be hanging out with his buddies. Not that that bothered her now that her sister was home.

They hadn't seen each other in over a year and yet their conversation was always casual, slipping between the important and the petty. Breast examinations. Nail polish. Bounced cheques. Vodka coolers. Tattoos. Her sister told her how, on her way to get groceries with her son, she commented that it wouldn't feel like a summer if she didn't walk barefoot along Cavendish Beach. Within hours they were packed and on the road.

"Where's Miles?" Trina asked

Her sister said their dad had taken him fishing. Whatever they caught they'd be having for supper.

That likely meant mackerel, Trina thought. Fried in butter.

"I forgot to ask, how long are you home?"

Her sister could only get a week off work and the drive would eat up most of her vacation. Until tomorrow, she said.

"Tomorrow," Trina repeated, trying to sound upbeat.

They had already passed the farm with the Shetland ponies. The purple house. The wooden bridge above the brook. As a girl she had reduced the trip to a series of landmarks, and just as they were coming up to the next one her sister eased on the brakes, smiling. Trina could see the white steeple. "No thanks," she said, laughing, once she started she couldn't stop. There was a time when she couldn't make the 24-mile drive without pestering her parents to stop at that church so that she could pee. The peeing church, her Mum called it.

About the same time they were able to see the water on the horizon they acknowledged with a glance the long dirt lane that led to the house they had grown up in.

"Was Mum surprised to see you?" Trina said.

Her sister said she seemed happy but not surprised. That before she even gave them a hug she began fixing a pot of tea.

"Sounds like her," Trina said.

Her sister then commented on how much their mom had aged.

"I'm sure even I'll notice a difference," Trina said. "I haven't been out there in a while."

"You got a kid, you work, you're busy," her sister said, coming to her defense.

"I am busy," she said, sighing as if she was tired and in need of a rest. The real reason she hardly ever visited her parents was because they didn't approve of Tony and she still thought it meant something to be a loyal wife.

Next came a motel, a gas station, a wax museum, and a graveyard that meant nothing to Trina now though someday it would.

Her sister pointed, a drift of sand from the dunes had reduced the road along the main beach down to one lane. She talked of how, if that kept up, there soon wouldn't be a road. That they'd have a long hike to get to the main beach.

"You drove across the country to be here," Trina said. "That would only slow you down."

With a sly smile her sister said that only erosion or death could keep her away. She was right and wrong. Death did keep her away. But so did the cancer. She died out in Calgary oblivious to the heat wave gripping the island, only her son and ex-husband at her side, her entire existence had been diminished to a bed in a ward in a huge hospital where cancer was as commonplace as crutches or pudding.

As soon as they got out of the car her sister made a show of breathing through her nose.

The salt air. The sweet smell of baking sand. The sky without a ceiling. The surf like a soft roar. The heavy heat diminished by a slight coastal breeze.

They had grown up just a mile down the road. No matter where their summer days began, they usually ended up at the beach. They climbed along the rocks at the base of the red cliffs featured in all the postcards. They let themselves be swept off their feet by the waves. They excavated crabs. Chased minnows. Collected beach glass and shells. And when they were tired from all of their adventuring they laid out on the dunes as soft as pillows, a quiet time to read or dream. Trina's big a kid at heart, so despite the difference in their ages always close.

On this last halcyon day, they stayed away from the crowded main beach, settling next to a salt-water stream that cut across the sand. They lugged grocery bags full of blankets, towels, lotions, toys, bags of chips and cold sweating bottles of Seaman's pop. They had this section of the beach all to themselves, only the gulls watching over them.

Miles showed up not long after they arrived. Mackerel, he confirmed. For the rest of the day he and Travis entertained themselves by playing in and along the stream, lugging rocks, looking for beached jellyfish.

As for Trina and her sister, they hardly spoke all afternoon. It wasn't that they didn't have anything to say. It was that they were as comfortable in silence as they were in conversation. And they understood how rare it was to get a day at the beach, the weather and their kids cooperating, their agendas their own.

Her sister went for a swim and several long walks, one that involved climbing along the rocks.

Trina lay in just about every possible position, adjusting the angle of her body as the sun slid west. Her goal was to get an even tan, to look good for Tony, the man whose name she had tattooed on her stomach. At one point she fell asleep and was woken by a gush of water. Christ, she yelled, ready to roar at Travis when she turned over and saw that it was her sister standing over her. She was holding a bucket, the boys at her back. Crazy laughter.

"I couldn't just let you burn," her sister said.

The day seemed to go on forever and yet when her sister mentioned they should go, supper's probably ready, Trina felt as if she had just heard the knock on her door. Twenty-six and sunny.

Back at her parents' place, she had the sort of meal she grew up on. Fried mackerel and a spoonful of mustard pickles. New potatoes, carrots, turnip, beets and their greens from the garden. A half a pound of butter in a porcelain dish. Bread pudding for dessert and while they drank brewed tea they stayed sitting at the table, too full to move.

Trina's sister had said their mom had aged but she didn't see it. As far as she was concerned, they all looked and acted younger as they reminisced while outside the day ended with the sky on fire, the sun falling into the sea.

10

The hospital was in the woods on the water with wide windows that framed the sort of peaceful scenery found in pictures hanging above wooden mantles in huge homes as old as countries. Not that Miles was in any state to appreciate the sight of willow trees drooping lazily over the red rocky edge of the river with its flat blue water. For him, the windows were torture and taunted him by making it seem like he was so close to peace when he felt far from it. He had thoughts of setting fire to the trees and polluting the river with ash, but when he shared these with one of the doctors they immediately upped the dosage on his medication.

He was in the psych ward. He kept to himself and his bed, refusing to use the wheelchair or crutches they provided. He stared out the window, the world now as foreign to him as on the day of his birth. And he slept as much as a newborn, overwhelmed by the strange sensation that he was sleeping even when awake.

During his stay he had three regular visitors. His aunt Trina cried every time she came to see him, usually before she even sat down across from him there were tears. He knew when she looked at him she saw her dead sister and tried not to see her own son, Travis. Grampy wouldn't cry until he got up to leave. I didn't mean to hurt your leg, he would always say, tears pooling in the folds of his face. And the first time Miles' cousin came to visit he was smiling like a cartoon devil, his hands behind his back.

"I have something to make you happy again," Travis said.

Miles almost managed a smile at the absurdity of that. He was sitting on his bed, trying to scratch beneath the metal brace on his broken leg.

"I'll give you three guesses," Travis said.

Normally Miles would've strung this game out, but there was nothing normal about where he was and how he felt and he said, "You got me a Happy Meal."

"How did you know?" Travis said.

"I could smell it."

Miles took the crinkled bag from Travis and looked inside. For a reason he couldn't explain, his heart sank and he felt that for the rest of his life he would be searching for something he'd never be able to find.

"Was this your idea?" Miles said.

"Yeah," Travis said. "Mum let me get one for you to make you happy again. I told her I wasn't happy either so I got one too."

The hamburger and the fries were dry and cold but the salt saved them and they were easily the best things Miles had eaten in a long time. When he looked up from his food, chewing, fending off dehydration with quick sips of fountain pop, he found Travis staring at him intently, as if he actually expected to see happiness spread across his face like morning sun.

"Are you happy now?" Travis said.

"I'm getting there," Miles said, stuffing the bag with garbage and handing Travis the toy, some wind-up car that had come with the meal.

Travis smiled and made the toy disappear. He looked around the room with its pale pink walls and white metal wire across a large window. It could've been a Barbie doll prison, at least that was Travis' first impression.

"Will they send me here when I stop being happy?" Travis said.

"You don't come here just because you're not happy," Miles said. He knew he had to keep it simple but didn't think he was doing Travis any favours by sheltering him from the truth. He told Travis about the voice in his head. How it didn't belong.

"How did it get there?" Travis said. "Did it break in?"

"I don't know."

"Crows break into my head. But don't tell anyone," Travis added. "I don't want them to send me here."

"I won't."

Travis nodded and said, "You might not know this but their eyes are better than binoculars. They can see right through our hair and skulls and into our brains."

It occurred to Miles that he probably sounded like that to other people. Blaming a voice in his head for why he showed up at his mom's grave with a shovel and started digging.

"Where's your mom?" Miles said.

"She's out in the car," Travis said.

"Tell her thanks."

"Okay."

Miles was anxious for Travis to go. He didn't know how much longer he could pretend and when the nurse showed up with her cart he was relieved, which was a first.

"Time to go," Miles said.

"Why?" Travis said.

"I have to take my pills."

"Pills for what?"

Miles made eye contact with the nurse and said, "That's what stops the voice from breaking into my head."

Travis seemed to think about this for a second. He looked back at the nurse. He walked up to Miles and cupped his hands around his ear and whispered, "Can they stop the crows from breaking into my head?"

"I don't know," Miles said. He really didn't know what else to say.

Miles was in the hospital for fifteen weeks, from July to the end of October. Six of them were dedicated to repairing his leg. The other nine focused on solving the mysteries of his mind. Each day he had a session with at least one of two doctors, sometimes both. Doctor #1 had narcolepsy, and at least once a session he would nod off and then startle himself awake. Doctor #2 had the soft soothing voice of a late-night disc jockey. He even dressed like one with his black mock turtlenecks and jeans. Since Miles refused to be mobile they conducted their sessions in his pink prison where they would ask him questions about his childhood, his family, particularly his mom, her cancer, his state of mind, and what sort of man he wanted to become. The disc jockey took plenty of notes. The narcoleptic would jot things down when he wasn't falling asleep. They were careful to avoid asking questions about the incident until the fourth week when he knew they felt they had established a "rapport" with him. All Miles could share with them was what Grampy told him had happened. He remembered nothing from the day of the incident, and very little of the weeks that preceded it. But he did remember the voice, how one day it showed up like an old friend who had traveled the world and had adopted such a strange new point of view that it was foreign while familiar. There was already a rapport. Miles could remember most of the conversations, just not days or events. For instance he didn't remember grabbing the shovel and setting out for his mom's grave, but he did recall the first time the voice broached the subject of his dead mother's final wish. The doctors never once reacted to what he said. Their only hint of a response came in how they adjusted the paper-cup cocktails of pills that the nurses delivered three times a day.

Miles was discharged with a set of crutches, a metal pin in his leg, five scrips for his meds and referrals to both a physiotherapist and a psychologist. The diagnosis, at least for the time being, was psychosis—though schizophrenia was mentioned.

Grampy was waiting to drive him home. Miles still hadn't forgiven him for what happened to his leg but had nowhere else to go. When his mom died he had moved in with Grampy. He slept in his mom's old bed and his clothes hung next to hers in the closet. She was buried almost halfway between the house and the white grassy dunes that guarded her favourite beach along the island's north shore.

When they were nearing home and Miles could finally see the familiar wedge of blue between the tops of the trees and the horizon he said, "There's one good thing that came out of this."

"What?" Grampy said, a smile slowly overwhelming his face like a yawn.

"I'm no longer afraid to die."

11

Lately Miles hadn't spent any more time in Grampy's house than he had to. Just as long as it took him to sleep and shower and eat and then he was out the door in his Doc Martens, hood up, walkman blaring. Sometimes he went straight to the tireless Malibu that was sunk into the ground, rooted like a tree at the back of the farm. Today he walked through the quiet woods, past boarded-up cottages, up the empty roads and down the long white beach that was eroding into the sea. It was November, just over a year since he got out of hospital. There was no wind. The leaves had long ago turned and were rotting in wet piles beneath the trees and all of the tourists were gone, everything closed, the town as lively as its graveyard. That's where his mom was. Next to her mom. He hardly ever visited them—he didn't see the point. But Grampy visited them so often he kept a lawn chair folded up behind their graves. He wasn't there today, but when Miles did find him there he'd watch him from the trees. Smoking, Grampy would talk to them about the weather, the gardens, how much wood he had in for the winter and when he got on the subject of Miles he sometimes cried. His crying sounded as if he were scraping his teeth across a chalkboard, and that was Miles' cue to slip his headphones back on and disappear into the trees.

He came to Chez Yvonne. The place he used to work. A house converted into a seafood restaurant named after the owner's old man's fishing boat. There was a blown-up picture of the boat behind the cash register, taken in 1977 from the wharf in Rustico. In the photo it was early morning, the day before lobster season and the deck was piled high with traps. The crew were bundled up and braced against the wind and the boat looked ready to topple as it ploughed through the white-capped waves out to sea. It sank that morning in the Gulf of St. Lawrence. The boat and the bodies were never found, chewed and swallowed by the hungry sea. And years later the sinking of that boat was the inspiration for a restaurant that fed the hungry with pillages from the sea. Miles washed dishes there, and at least once a shift he'd come out from that sauna of a kitchen for a look. Such a fearless picture of men who risked and lost everything in an attempt to earn a buck, it would inspire him to get through his shifts: ten hours of steam, sweat, and soggy skin and clothes that stank of cheap dish soap, fried oil and stale fish. It helped him get through the summer: this was the longest he held down a job since his mom died. Thanks to that picture he now worked for the government. Not really, but sort of, since they sent him a cheque every two weeks. They were paying him to do nothing because he worked all summer long. When the woman at the employment office told him he would have enough weeks to qualify for EI, he raised his arms in the air as if he had completed a marathon. And on the last day the restaurant was open for the season, the owner and cook, Paul, told Miles over his shoulder and the sizzle of haddock frying in butter and onions that he had a job there next summer if he wanted. He even mentioned promoting him to prep cook. After Paul served up the haddock they shook hands like men. For the first time in a long while Miles felt like he had it under control. That he was in charge of his head and his life. That he could stop living like an alcoholic, one day at a time. As normal twenty-year-olds do, he began making plans for his future.

He walked across the cracked parking lot, up the five steps. The door was boarded up. So were the windows but when he leaned over the railing he could see through a crack in he boards and into the restaurant. The chairs and tables were stacked in the corner. The cash register was open. Empty. And he could only see the outline of the frame on the wall behind it. No Chez Yvonne, just a shadow.

He was overwhelmed by a suffocating loneliness and thought this was how it felt to drown.

He had a metal pin in his leg. He walked until he could feel it scraping against the underside of his knee and then he turned back. The sky was grey white with yellow smudges, the colours of an old undershirt. Stray leaves were stuck to the empty road and foxes were the only traffic he had seen for days.

By the time he got to the mailbox at the end of Grampy's lane he could feel his heart pumping blood. He pulled out the familiar brown envelope. He read his name. This was what he had been waiting for all last week and still he was caught by surprise. Overwhelmed. He had been telling himself that the day he received it he would say his piece and five minutes later be gone like the last bit of light at dusk. He figured that would hurt the most, and he wanted Grampy to suffer like he did when he opened the mailbox a couple months back, discovering just how alone he was in the world.

Miles needed to settle his head and his heart, firm up his plan and so he hobbled down the red dirt lane, heading for the Malibu. He passed Grampy's house. Two stories, sunflower yellow with a perennial garden out front that was in bloom from spring to early fall. Not the sort of house anyone would've expected Grampy to live in, for thirty-five years he was a janitor at a school. He grew his own root vegetables. He kept chickens and cows that he had slaughtered. He heated his house and barn with dead trees and discarded pallets and he cooled his beer in a damp hole he'd dug in the ground. A man of the land as practical as a shovel, it was his wife who picked the colour of the house and planted the perennials. She had been dead for years and he still couldn't seem to betray what she started. Miles on the other hand was alive, more like a son then grandson he was told, and Grampy had no problem betraying him.

He passed the house and noticed Grampy out back. Grampy was holding a chainsaw, leaning over a pallet that he was cutting up for kindling. Now he was looking up, his mouth moving, but all Miles heard was his rap music. Six Feet Deep, a song about a crew of gangbangers, how each of them ended up dead and in the ground. Miles ignored Grampy and kept walking, his eyes on the sinking car.

The red Malibu was facing the woods, next to a tree that had dropped its apples. They were scattered on the ground, gnawed at, rusty brown like the body of the car. And there was mould in the backseat. Spider webs in the corners. Leather flaking off the dash and the key still in the ignition. It would torment him. If only I was the turn of a key away from escaping this place, he would think.

He got into the car. It smelled sweet, of yesterday's sun and the faded vanilla air freshener hanging from the rearview mirror. It wasn't much warmer there than outside, but at least it was shelter, and not Grampy's. It had belonged to his mom, and she had left everything to him. It was her first car. He tried not to think about all the firsts it was home to. He tried to not think about his past, the moving around, the divorce, death, mayhem in his head and heart. Dr. Tweel kept telling him to take it one day at a time. For a while he listened: his office walls were crowded with degrees, awards and certificates, proof of just how much he knew. One day, one pill at a time, that was always the last thing he said to Miles before he left his office for another four weeks out in the world.

Miles was watching the poplars sway when he felt cold air on his side. He looked over. Grampy was holding the car door open. He was stocky, bald on top, his skin wrinkled and windburnt and he was wearing a blue green plaid coat sprayed with woodchips.

"What?" Miles said, not bothering to stop his walkman.

He pulled Miles' hood back, ripped the headphones from his ears and holding them, his hands shaking, he said, "I'm sick of being ignored."

Ears ringing, Miles shrugged his shoulders.

"And what's wrong with the house?" Grampy said. "Why are you always out here?"

"I want my headphones back," Miles said.

"Not until you talk."

"I am talking to you. Hand them over."

"Enough," he said, his face red and sagging, looking ready to collapse like an old abandoned barn. Grampy hadn't always been that way, emotional, but something changed in him when he buried his daughter soon after his wife.

"I know what's going on," Grampy said. There were tears in his eyes.

Miles' stomach sank.

"I know," he said again, and Miles watched as a tear fell from his eye. It got caught in a crease in his cheek, as deep as a ravine that emptied at the corner of his mouth. Miles knew what would be coming next. The ravine would be overflowing, Grampy would be choking on tears while he had him trapped in the car and though he wanted to see him suffer he hated to see him cry. Grampy's old barn of a face would collapse into a heap of corroded nails and curling shingles and rotting wood while an awful scraping sound would come from deep inside his throat.

"Good for you," Miles said. "So you know. Big deal. I'm going."

Grampy stared at him with wide empty eyes. Miles had the feeling he had caught him by surprise. That Grampy was talking about something else, medication maybe, and that he didn't know about him leaving.

"Where exactly are you going?" Grampy said.

"Away," Miles said.

"Where away?"

"Wherever."

"And what will you do."

"Whatever it takes."

"Where will you stay?"

"Somewhere with a roof."

Grampy glanced down at the toes of his work boots, steel showing through. He rubbed his eyes. "It doesn't seem like you put much thought into this," he said.

"All I do is think about it," Miles said. "The way I see it I can go anywhere."

"You can't do this," Grampy said, and through his anger he regained his voice. "No, you need family around. People watching over you. People who are familiar with your situation."

"Situation?" he said.

"You know what you got. There's no sense in reminding you."

"Well I think the country isn't good for somebody in your situation."

"What's that supposed to mean?"

"They're dead, but you go on visiting them and talking to them as if they are alive."

"I'm coping."

"Barely."

"What do you know?"

"A helluva lot more than you think."

Grampy got quiet.

Miles' jaw was shaking.

"Mom wasn't even in the ground when you told me I could come live with you," Miles said. "You told me that your home would always be my home and that even though you weren't my dad you would be there for me like one. I believed you. I trusted you. I know you've been contacting group homes. Discussing my situation. I know you want to get rid of me and that's why I'm going."

"Group homes? What gave you that idea?"

"I might have a situation but I can still read mail."

Grampy got quiet, his face froze.

Miles grabbed his headphones. Before Grampy could react he slammed the door. He locked it. He locked all the doors and then he was back to his music, hood and volume up, eyes shut so tight that he didn't know whether he was hearing the song or Grampy banging on the car. Maybe it was a bit of both, either way he didn't care.

Miles opened his eyes. No Grampy. The wind had picked up. The clouds had parted, they were large and grey and sliding across the sky and the poplars were flailing. He changed tapes, going from Ghetto Boys to Bob Dylan. He thought of Grampy, how it may have been more of his bullshit but that he liked what he said about him having a situation. It sounded better than a condition. Less permanent. Something he could overcome without the help of a pill.

Dr. Tweel called what he had a condition of the mind that altered the way he perceived and reacted to the world around him. According to Dr. Tweel, because of his condition he couldn't tell the difference between what was happening in and outside of his head and so he created his own realities. The realities were often confusing, full of conflict, cruel even. This was a painful way to live, Dr. Tweel told him, but told him there were ways he could ease the pain. Dr. Tweel spoke casually, as if what he was asking Miles to do was as natural as drinking water, and said all

Miles had to do was take the medication Dr. Tweel prescribed. What he failed to mention was that Miles would have to take the medication every day for the rest of his life. Every day the same taste in his throat like burning chalk.

"The aftertaste is normal," Dr. Tweel said. "It is a sign that the pill is dissolving, doing its job."

"When I take the pills I feel different," Miles said. "The only way I can describe it is that I feel less like myself. I don't know where I end and the pills begin."

"That could be said of anything in our lives," he said. "Take coffee for instance. Every morning I find it hard to determine where I end and the coffee begins."

"That isn't the same," Miles said. "Everybody drinks coffee."

"You don't," he said.

Dr. Tweel was tall, bald with round gold glasses and yellow skin with brown spots that matched the cardigan he seemed to be always wearing. He looked like a grandfather from a movie. Miles had trusted him like one up until four weeks ago when he told him he had good news.

"I always like good news," Dr. Tweel said, grabbing from his desk a round glass paperweight. He held it near his leg, shuffling it in his hand like a pitcher searching for the seams on a baseball.

"I'm better," Miles said.

"Certainly. You are doing much better."

"I don't think you understand."

"I do. You just need to remember that better is relative."

"I don't need any more of your medication."

"We've been through this before."

"This time it's different."

"How?"

"It just is. I'm older. I got experience. I can control it now."

"And the best chance of staying in control is to continue taking your medication and coming to therapy. What you have, there's no cure."

Miles knew he was going to say something like that. If all of Dr. Tweel's patients were cured he'd be out of a job and so it was in his own best interest to say that the diseases he treated were incurable. Miles tried to imagine a mechanic pulling that, saying that the car was irreparable and that your only hope of keeping it on the road was if you bought special gas and brought it back every four weeks for a checkup.

"I'm sorry," Dr. Tweel said, setting down the paperweight. He picked up a pad and a pen.

"What are you writing?" Miles said.

"I always take notes."

"I want to see what you're writing this time."

"I'm sorry but my notes are private."

"I want a pen and paper. I think I'll take some notes of my own."

He ignored his request and kept writing.

"Stop," Miles yelled.

Dr. Tweel looked at Miles over the top of his glasses like a stern old teacher who believed he had seen it all and then some and that gave him the right.

"Don't look at me like that," Miles said.

"I'm looking at you with concern," he said.

"Well I'm looking at you with disgust."

Dr. Tweel wrote some more and when his pen stopped moving his mouth started, "I notice a drastic change in your behavior. I want you to answer me honestly."

Miles already knew what he was going to ask. That was one of the worst things about his situation. He couldn't get angry, sad or confused without somebody thinking he was off his medication. The way he saw it, everybody pretended they were so sad he wasn't normal but the second he started acting normal everybody got paranoid. Irrational. They looked into every little thing he did as a symptom, a sign, a red sky warning of bad weather brewing and yet he was the one with the label.

Miles reached across the desk and grabbed the glass paperweight. He brought it back behind his head.

"Miles," Dr. Tweel managed to say.

Miles flung his hand forward.

Dr. Tweel flinched, raising his arms to cover his face. Slowly he opened his eyes, staring at Miles from behind his bony arms.

Miles got up to go and instead of the usual line, the one day one pill at a time bullshit, Dr. Tweel said, "I'm not trying to scare you but it will get worse. You'll withdraw deeper into yourself. If the voice comes back it will be louder, more persistent. Your anger will turn to rage. Every time we go to war we lose more of ourselves. And we can only handle so much war," he said as Miles slammed the office door behind him, still holding the paperweight that he dropped in the garbage in the lobby. As soon as his fingers let go he felt as light as a kite.

Miles spent most of the day sitting in the Malibu, trying to get up the nerve to go while listening to Dylan sing about the wind and change and heaven's door in hopes that it would inspire him. It didn't. He had begun to doubt if he'd ever go. He had begun to wonder if in fifty years he would be the one living by himself in this graveyard of a town, talking to the dead from a lawn chair, wood chips in his hair.

The light was fading. The temperature had dropped. His breath was like smoke in the grey fall air and Dylan's voice was slow and heavy, the batteries in his walkman dying. When his mom was dying, her hair like a dried-up plant, skin shrink-wrapped to her bones and her body so numb from the drugs that her mouth hardly moved when she spoke, she tried to give him advice and encouragement to last a lifetime.

One of the last things she told him—she didn't know he was sick at that point, nobody did—was to live. Really live, she said, Woodstock only comes once.

His mom loved music. Joplin, Hendrix, she saw both of them at Woodstock when she was sixteen, having gone on an impulse, seven friends in a car with just the clothes on their backs and a hundred bucks between them. She never lost her spontaneity. One summer when they were out in Calgary in a heat wave on their way to the grocery store she started talking about how much she missed her family and the white-hot sand of Cavendish Beach. Hours later they were crossing Saskatchewan, Joplin screeching, heading home for a vacation.

His mom died. Cancer. He still found it hard to think of her down there, an eternity of stale dirt and darkness for a woman who loved sand and sun so much.

His mom went and his symptoms came in the form of a voice, low and steady like a hum. It knew the past. The future. It knew what people were hiding from him, what they would've told him if they hadn't lost their voices with their lives. It seemed to know everything and he believed it as if it were God himself (for a brief while he thought it was). And when it told him that all his mom wanted, her final wish, was for him to bring her to the beach, he responded as any good son would.

It just happened that Grampy drove past the graveyard as Miles was stabbing the shovel into the ground. Grampy stopped the car and when he tried to take the shovel Miles grunted and jabbed him in the chest with the blade and then went back to digging, relaxed but determined, so that Grampy had to tackle him. Miles fell on the shovel, his shin shoving against the blade until it cracked under their weight. All of this went on while a few headstones down a group of Asians, a busload of them, clicked pictures and posed in front of L.M. Montgomery's gravesite.

That day was vague in his memory, and when Grampy told him what happened he felt as if a sober friend was reminding him of what he said and did one drunken night.

Two surgeries and morphine and one metal pin later and they were able to fix his leg. Over a year of doctors and tests and metal beds in white rooms and pills that were supposed to make him better, but instead they made him apathetic and fat and twitchy and his shit poured out of him like hot butter and his gums were so dry and sensitive that chewing toast felt like eating shards of glass but in the end they silenced the voice.

They won.

He lost. The highlight of the last year had been ten weeks of washing dishes.

He wanted to have sex again. To get high and drunk: both were forbidden while on medication. He wanted friends and memories. He wanted to do something with his life, have a good time doing it and he knew his mom would want it that way. Inspired, he opened the car door, his plan was to pack and then hobble the five shivering hours to town. He had a picture in his mind of Terry Fox.

There was no sign of Grampy in the house. Miles packed quickly and was halfway down the lane when he saw Grampy up ahead. A dark shape in the blue grey light coming towards him.

"When she was dying I was dying along with her," Grampy yelled. "Inside anyway. But you want to know what saved me?

You. When she asked me to take care of you everything changed. I knew I had to be strong for somebody. Because of you I was able to keep going."

Miles wished the darkness was thick enough that he could hide from Grampy's eyes. They were desperate, pleading.

"I did contact a few group homes," Grampy said. "It was Dr. Tweel's idea. You're twenty. He thought it would be a good way to transition you from living with me to being out on your own."

"I don't care about Dr. Tweel," Miles said. "You betrayed me."

"I just wanted what was best for you."

"It doesn't matter anymore. Woodstock only comes once," Miles said, and when he walked around Grampy he saw that he was holding a folded chair. The one from the graveyard.

"Do you have your medication?" Grampy said.

"I'm sure you've been talking to your good buddy Dr. Tweel," Miles said.

"I have."

"Well?"

"I was hoping you changed your mind."

Miles kept walking while listening to the crows plot and the wind bully the trees. The town was restless, and for the first time in months it felt alive.

"Please tell me where you're going," Grampy said.

Miles didn't know where he was going. Charlottetown to Moncton. Moncton to wherever. He thought about telling Grampy as much but in the end he didn't. He said, which was more than he had planned on sharing, "I'm catching a bus."

"At least let me drive you to town," Grampy said.

If it weren't for his leg, the one Grampy broke, he would've ignored him and kept walking, quietly afraid, his heart pounding.

The parking lot glowed yellow. Early evening but it was already dark. Not near as windy as on the North Shore. Cold enough to snow. As Miles got out of the car Grampy tried to make a big production out of the goodbye but it was a one-man show. Miles heaved his bag over his shoulder and headed towards the apartment building. About twelve units, it looked like a mushroom that was shriveling, past its prime in a scabby field. Miles got Grampy to drop him off at his Aunt Trina's. It was close enough to the bus station. He wanted to say goodbye.

The building smelled of old carpet and Kraft Dinner. He walked down the narrow wood-paneled stairway to the basement. He heard talking coming from behind thin walls. Their apartment was at the end of the hall. The door was halfway open. He didn't knock.

The room had a blue TV glow. The volume was down. The heat was up and Aunt Trina was lying on her side on the sofa, passed out or asleep, the musk of old alcohol hanging heavy in the air.

"Trina," he said.

Nothing.

"Trina," he said louder, touching her shoulder.

Without even opening her eyes she said, "Get." He knew she thought he was Travis. She was another one who hadn't been the same since his mom died. And she only got worse when Uncle Tony went to jail, the end of their marriage coming not long after.

Miles walked down the hall to Travis' room. The door was closed. Knowing Travis he knocked. No answer. He pushed open the door. There was a mattress on the floor. No sheets, it was as floral and yellowed as old wallpaper. There were empty ketchup packets on the floor.

The state of the mattress and the quantity of ketchup packets didn't surprise him. If anything, he was expecting worse. The last time he had opened the door to Travis' room he had been swarmed by what turned out to be the stench of dead animal.

They came from a small family. Two sisters, two kids and a set of grandparents. Miles was older than Travis, the closest thing each of them had to a brother. Miles tried to look out for him. Give Travis advice when he could. He never held back, sharing with Travis what he had been through so Travis would know he wasn't alone. Miles knew he had it bad but felt Travis had it a thousand times worse. Travis had been to doctors but because of his age and his range of symptoms they couldn't pinpoint what it was. At least not yet. It didn't help that Trina denied that there was anything wrong. Miles once heard her say, "He's different, I know that. But he's at a confusing age. Some just struggle with finding themselves." Miles knew she was right to an extent. Some struggle. But then some, like he and Travis, went to war with themselves.

Miles wanted to wait for Travis, say goodbye, but the last bus of the evening would be leaving shortly and he still needed to get batteries for his walkman. Music can drown out almost any voice, real or imagined.

When he looked at Trina he sometimes saw his mom. In a certain light, at the right angle. Not tonight. He gave her a kiss on the cheek. She stirred but didn't wake.

Outside it was snowing. Snow as fine as salt fell quietly through the black sky, through the bare arms of trees, through the branches that stretched out over the road like long fingers. Suddenly he felt as if he wasn't alone. He stopped walking and scanned the shadows of trees and the dark parking lot.

"Travis," Miles said, because his cousin had been known to follow people. He was sure he had killed small animals and he knew he thought he was a spy.

"Travis," he said again.

The snow felt like sparks against his skin.

There was no reply, Travis or otherwise.

12

He could've got off anywhere. Moncton. Trois-Riviéres. Toronto. Steinbeck. Medicine Hat. The second largest country in the world and he had enough money to take him anywhere he wanted to go. But as he rode the bus through concrete cities and towns as ordinary as pennies he became afraid to commit to starting a life in a place he'd been for no longer than an hour, as long as it took to unload, to board, for the bus driver to fit in a smoke and a piss. So by the time he reached the prairies he had a good idea where he was going to end up.

The bus pulled into Calgary and it was snowing, the flakes melting as fast as they fell. The pavement was dark and wet. The city was crammed with cars and people and buildings that crowded the sky like the nearby Rockies. Calgary was bigger and busier than he had remembered. He had lived here for over ten years. He and his mom followed his dad when he got a job as a roughneck on a drill rig. His dad was gone more than he was around. His mom couldn't live like that and left him. His dad was still out here and from what Miles knew he was now a driller on a rig and in charge of his own crew, rarely around but when he was in town he never left the clubs, a wad of cash buying him all the friends and drugs and women he wanted.

They barely spoke. It was hard to talk to someone who only cared about himself and was always out in the bush. At some point he planned on trying to get ahold of him. He thought he might even ask if he could stay at his place for a while until he found a job. For now he wanted to find a room with a bed where he could leave his bag. Sleep. Hopefully screw. It was nearly two years since he had been with a girl. He'd spent so much time wrestling with one of his heads that he ignored the other.

Headphones blaring, he left the bus station and walked towards 7th Avenue. The streets were familiar in where they took him. Everything else about them was foreign: the frenzy of shapes, colours, and faces that stared right through him as if he wasn't there. He felt like a ghost wandering the busy streets of a city he had been to when he'd been alive. That he could go anywhere but be a part of nothing. See without being seen. He thought he would feel different here but this was exactly how he felt back in PEI. A ghost of a man haunting a world in which he didn't belong.

The first hotel he came by, he knew by the chandelier, was more than he wanted to spend. He passed more places with revolving gold doors and glowing lobbies and he didn't even bother checking the prices. The buildings shrank and the traffic thinned before he came across the Owl's Nest Motel, a long white bungalow shaped like an L and on its wooden sun-faded sign there was a picture of a familiar black owl wearing a robe and slippers. It watched him with wide yellow eyes like it had been doing since he first saw it in Northern New Brunswick, perched on a power line above a bleak stretch of highway. The owl in one form or another had followed him out West. He had seen it on T-shirts, tree branches, candy wrappers, restaurants and now on a motel sign. He wasn't sure where he stood with God but he thought of it as his guardian angel. It knew he was in danger. He was sure it kept watch when he slept. It now wanted him to stay in one of its nests where it could keep an eye on him. And Miles knew he could use an extra set of eyes.

"I'd like a room," he said.

A blond with a perm and purple eye shadow sat behind the desk, painting her nails. "For the night?" she said, without looking up.

He nodded, not wanting to say out loud how long he wanted to stay.

She kept on painting her fingernails, still without looking at him. "I'm the one getting paid to sit here," she said. "I got all day."

He checked over his shoulder. "How much for six nights?" he whispered.

She told him.

He paid her for two.

At that price he wasn't expecting much. There was brown carpet that had lost its shag in most places, heavy green curtains that blocked out the light, a velvet picture of a dusky forest above the bed. In a way the room reminded him of a nest. There was a small TV and he went through the channels. Grampy didn't have cable, and part of him would've liked to stay in the room for the rest of the day and night and watch other people's memorable lives flick brightly by while his remained as dreary and loveless as a slug's. But the thing was he was there to make new memories.

The last time he came to visit, having just turned eighteen, his dad took him to Bikini Beach. Two of the strippers knew his dad by name, not that that surprised him. With a whisper and a handshake his dad arranged for one of them to give Miles a private dance. Her name was Mercedes. Her dark hair shone like chrome, she had a nose ring, dimples, a baby's smooth round belly and her outfit, or lack of one, was the colour of pink bubblegum. She was not quite innocent, but almost. She took him by the hand and led him through a curtain into a stall and by the time he took a seat her eyes were closed and she was swaying to the music, grinding her ass into his lap, sliding off her top and bottoms so that he could watch her rub her nipples and touch between her legs and at one point she spread herself open just inches from his face so that he could almost taste her on his tongue, damp and salty like the sea. She whispered in his ear that for an extra twenty she'd jerk him off. She went at him with a mouthful of saliva and two calloused hands and it took all of thirty seconds. He couldn't have done it better himself.

He thought of Mercedes often. And not just when he masturbated. He hoped she was still working there. Though that was a couple years ago. He knew a lot could change in that time. He had lost his mom and his sanity. He could only imagine what she had lost by selling her body day in day out to people like his dad for cash or drugs that helped her get through the spotlight nights and the dark early mornings that followed.

It had stopped snowing. It was a wet cold afternoon and Miles' headphones were wrapped around his neck so he could hear tires grate against cement as the cab pulled away leaving him standing in the near empty parking lot. On the side of the brick building was a huge set of cartoon tits barely covered by a string bikini. Soggy cigarette butts were mashed into the cement outside of the tinted door.

A dark wooden hallway with posters of current performers, but no Mercedes, led into an open room and at the centre of it an elevated stage with a spotlight and a pole. There were chairs around the edge of the stage and then rows of tables and a sandbox and a bar in the back corner. There was nobody dancing at the moment—just dance music. There was nobody there except for a few unhappy-looking men, all of them staring at the same small sandy blond in a white fishnet dress and chunky black heels who was talking to a bartender. He had yellow highlights in his hair. He was almost as wide as he was tall and Miles thought he could use some chunky heels of is own.

Miles approached the bar.

In a southern drawl the blond complained to the bartender how she was there a month and still working days. "Days lick ass," she said, noticing Miles. She was young, her face a fresh piece of paper and she gave him a once-over with her dressed up eyes.

"Like you have to tell me," the bartender said. He also gave Miles a once-over.

She continued, "The men that are here during the day, they don't work. They barely got money for drinks and tips, let alone lap dances. And when I told Ricky I wanted to work a few extra shifts, nights, to earn the money that I'm short on my rent, get some dances under my belt, you know, he told me I wasn't ready. How the fuck am I supposed to get ready if I don't get any practice?" she said, again glancing Miles' way and he wondered if she was sending him a hint.

"You can practice on me," the bartender said.

She bit her lip. "Is Rhonda working tonight?" she asked.

"Until close. How about it?"

"How about you do your job," she said, looking at Miles. "Card him, he doesn't look a day over sixteen," she said with the confident smile of a girl who knew just how attractive she was, the devotion her body inspired. She turned. Through her dress he could see her black thong drop down into the depths of her ass and he thought of the boat the restaurant where he'd worked all summer was named after, all by itself at the bottom of the sea. She disappeared behind a door marked private that blended with the wooden wall.

"You heard the girl," the bartender said. "ID."

Miles wanted to order a beer but knew he needed to stay sharp. "Root beer," he said.

"Root beer," the bartender said.

"Yeah."

"Root beer," the bartender said again, smiling. "Want a straw with that?"

Miles paid. He asked the bartender if he knew Mercedes.

"I used to fuck Mercedes. So yeah, I think I know her."

"When does she work next?"

"Buddy, she's been gone over a year."

"Gone where?"

"I can't see that that's any of your business."

"I met her once. She was special."

"They're all special when they're taking off their clothes."

"I don't believe that."

"You spend enough time here and you will," he said. The bartender was old enough to be his father; Miles could see it in his skin dried out like a dirt road that was beginning to crack. He was wearing a thick gold wedding band. Greenish letters were tattooed along his knuckles. He went back to emptying the dishwasher.

Miles sat at a table with a view of the stage and the door marked private. His pop fizzled. There would be no almost tasting Mercedes on his tongue. No spitting on his dick for lubrication. No convincing her to come back to his room after her shift and he might've been crushed if he hadn't just encountered the girl in the white fishnet dress. He was buoyed by the fact that she had noticed him. Her drawl like lazy sex. He imagined her soft hands. Her swollen lips. She needed money, which he had.

As he waited for her to reappear he saw the dark shape of the owl up where the spotlights were. It was nice to have it close. It opened its yellow eyes. Like high beams they cut through the grubby dark and lit the stage like they would an open highway. The music stopped mid-song.

"Back for her last set," said a voice through the speakers. "A sexy little thing from Texas out here in the wild Canadian west. Dallas!"

The door that she had disappeared behind flew open. She strutted out wearing a different outfit, something skimpy and dark, and she now wore a cowboy hat and she was holding a plastic cap gun. She blew kisses as she shot the unhappy looking men with a bang bang bang and oddly enough being shot was what it took to get a smile out of them. She forgot to shoot Miles. He wasn't sure how to feel about that as she stepped into the dusty light. A glow came off her hair. Her song came on. It was familiar. A rock western. It began by mentioning a weary head, being lost, God, the Devil, a lover, a candle in the wind. Miles felt the song was about his trip out west, and hoped the part about the lover was about to come true.

She began dancing but there was no building with the music. No flow. From the gate she galloped around the stage like a wound-up filly. She lunged from the spotlight to the pole to the edge of the stage and back again for a second lap while she ripped off her clothes as if they were on fire. Halfway through the song she was wearing only chunky heels, lying on her stomach, reaching under herself, spreading her lips. She bucked lazily as the song climaxed and then suddenly she stood. The song was not finished but she seemed to be. Chocolate nipples, firm curves, the V of trim blond pubic hair were on perfect display until the music stopped.

Her second song was more of the same, only it involved a stint in the sandbox where, for almost a minute, she seemed to have forgotten she was performing and sulked in the sand like a teenager on vacation with her parents. When she was done she collected her clothes and gun and with a bang bang wink (she winked in Miles' direction, which meant so much more to him than an empty gunshot) she hurried off the stage and through the same door through which she'd entered.

It was obvious why her boss felt she wasn't ready for nights. But she was beautiful, Miles thought, and with a little practice...

The stage went dark. He remembered the owl. It was gone from its perch. He searched the room. He was met with shadows like the ones that had filled the restaurant after it was boarded up for the winter. The shadows were as thick as steaks. Easy to hide behind. A frightening thought for him.

He may have been able to silence the voice in his head with music, but that no longer mattered. He was being guarded by an owl but stalked by a face that was white and doughy, all forehead, no hair, no eyebrows and the mouth of a barracuda. The sort of face that had him believing in God because after looking it in the eye he needed to know that there was something that stood for good.

As Miles made his way across the country he began too see the face on all sorts of bodies, in cars and on sidewalks, and the last time he saw it it boarded his bus. Sat two seats ahead of him. It wore a long grey trench coat. It smelled of fish. In its blue-veined hand it held a bible-like book with a black leather cover and a rusty zipper to protect its gold-tipped pages. The whole ride it read. Jagged lips moving but otherwise it was as still as a house. When the bus pulled into the next station it zipped up its book, flakes of rust falling down onto its lap. It turned and stared at Miles. Flashed him a barracuda smile and said, I will always find you.

Miles finished his root beer.

He was growing impatient for Dallas to come out from behind the door. He was hoping she still had some shift left and would come right up to him and ask if he'd like a private dance. Of course he would say yes. And depending on how things went he thought he would suggest a change of venue. The Owl's Nest, so that he could feel somewhat safe and enjoy himself like he had with Mercedes. If it's a question of money, he planned on saying, let's just say I have your rent covered. And you can practice.

The door opened. Out walked a woman who was much older than Dallas, her hair black with blond zebra stripes, her dress a hybrid of several different animal prints. She walked up to the bartender. She was taller than him and touched his neck, her fingers creeping up through his hair and down his back with familiar affection. It was obvious they were together. She was the Rhonda who worked nights, freeing him up to hit on young strippers.

Miles decided he couldn't wait any longer. He needed to find Dallas before the face found him or the bartender found her.

The place had emptied. The unhappy-looking men were either outside smoking or already on their way back to the lives they had briefly escaped. Before opening the door marked private he made sure the bartender wasn't watching him. Rhonda was asking him a question he didn't seem to want to answer as he counted change on the back counter.

Through the door was a short hallway that led into a bright open room. It smelled like a Sears perfume counter. There was a large mirror. There was a wall of lockers and in front of them a wooden bench where two women sat with their backs to him. One of them seemed to be dressed as a cheerleader. The other was Dallas. Her feet were bare, she was wearing faded jeans that hung low on her hips and a shear black bra. He found her even more attractive half-clothed than when she was up on stage bearing it all. He credited her bra, its dark iridescence like something alive in deep water. He always had a thing for sheer, how it could transform the most boring of body parts into places he wanted to lick like ice cream and he felt it was more than just a coincidence. Dallas wore that bra with him in mind. Somehow she knew.

Miles hesitated before saying, "You winked at me."

Dallas turned. She was wide-eyed. Silent.

"You didn't shoot me," he said. "I was a little hurt until you winked at me," he said, and that was when he noticed that the cheerleader, dirty blond curls down to her shoulders, had the mouth of a barracuda. Pale skin. Bloodshot eyes.

He felt himself backing up.

Too late, it said, low and steady like a hum.

The same voice that had been inside of his head, that he was able to silence until now, belonged to the face that had followed him across the country. One way or another, he realized, it would get to him and everybody he cared about.

"Leave us alone," Miles said. "Please, I'm begging you."

Dallas looked from him to the face, her eyes now screaming for help and an awful sound came from deep within her throat.

"Run," he yelled. "Dallas, run, run, run."

He couldn't understand why she grabbed on to the enemy and held it, still screaming. He got the feeling that she was afraid of him. That she thought of him as the enemy.

Arms like vice grips wrapped around his neck. They squeezed, choking him. They dragged him through the club and dropped him outside on the wet cold cement. He could hear and feel plastic cracking against his hip. He was stomped on, crushed like the thousands of cigarettes that formed a pulp where he lay.

He couldn't catch his breath. He hurt all over, the pain magnified by the cold and he counted three sets of boots. He looked up. The bartender was standing next to two of the unhappy looking men with their sandpaper faces. They were grinning. They seemed to enjoy beating him as much as they enjoyed being shot with a cap gun by a stripper.

"You piece of shit pervert," said the bartender. "I see you here again and I won't be so friendly."

Between breaths Miles managed to say, "She winked at me."

He sighed. "You crazy fuck," he said. "She winked at me. I'm the one fucking her."

Laughter. Another stomp, it felt different than the others, there was more edge to the heel. The bartender had already gone inside and one of the unhappy looking men was standing over him. A cigarette pressed between his lips, he was the picture of happiness.

The cover was gone from his walkman but it still played if he held it so that the tape was facing up. Not that that really mattered anymore. Music was powerless, just a bunch of empty words and sounds. And he felt powerless as he stood in the darkening parking lot outside a convenience store, holding a broken walkman in one hand and a receiver from a pay phone in the other. It was cold. He was huddled into the phone as it rang while cars and trucks raced by on the double-lane highway, weaving, their engines snarling like rabid dogs and the exhaust burning the soft skin inside his nose.

The operator said Miles' name, asked the person on the other end of the line if they'd accept the charges.

"Of course," Grampy said, his voice like a warm bath. Instantly Miles was comforted.

"Hey."

"Where are you?"

Miles could hear the worry in his voice. He told him exactly where he was. Grampy had more questions and unlike the last time they talked Miles answered them all. He even told him about the owl, the face, the incident at the strip club and how he wandered for almost an hour until he found a pay phone.

"I know it isn't fair," Grampy said. "It's dead wrong, but you're vulnerable."

"Yeah," Miles said, tired of the fight and he let go of the tears that had been building in his eyes since he first heard Grampy's voice. They dropped down his cheeks, the warm tears of defeat.

"Have you been to see your dad?" Grampy said.

"I don't even know if he's in town."

"You know what I think of him. But right now, out there, he's all that you got. I want you to try and get in touch with him and I'll contact Dr. Tweel. He'll know what to do. He'll help us," he said, his voice cracking like the logs in the fire that Miles knew was burning in the cast iron stove next to Grampy who wore a plaid coat two sizes too large, long johns and thick grey woolen socks. Miles knew the house now smelled of burning wood and stewing turnip and beef and that the sun was gone but the light above the kitchen table was on where the paper lay open. It was thin with news but covered the island like the dew and Miles would've traded all the money in his wallet to be there right now.

"What do you think?" Grampy said.

"Even if he's in town I don't want to see Dad," Miles said.

"Then go back to your motel but I want you to call me as soon as you get there. In the meantime I'll make a few calls."

"I thought things would be different here. That I would feel better about myself. My life. The truth is I feel worse. Calgary may be full of people but it's an empty place."

"It took your mom years to realize that. It would never be home."

"Grampy, I want to come home."

"It isn't much of a home without you."

Miles gave the cab driver the address for his motel. The driver was wearing a turban and without a word he pulled out of the convenience store parking lot and headed back in the direction of Bikini Beach. They were on the outskirts of the city, traffic was flowing like the Bow River and they passed a dark vacant lot where yellow machinery sat rusted and unused next to a deep hole in the ground. They passed places with fluorescent signs that sold car parts, concrete, cash, gas, and plumbing supplies. They passed empty unlit buildings with the markings of failed businesses. They passed pubs and restaurants, their fluorescent signs bigger and brighter than the ones that came before them and they shone in the night sky like flares trying to get people to come save them because like people they were all struggling to survive in a city that was as indifferent to human life as the nearby mountains. Miles could no longer see the mountains as they blended with the Coke-coloured sky but he knew that they were there, cruel and callous like the sea that was home to sunken boats, lost lives, barracudas and roaming legions of jellyfish that would wash up on to the north shore. Miles and his cousin Travis used to drop heavy red rocks on jellyfish and then dodge the splatter. After they destroyed one they would celebrate like linebackers having just made a tackle. They were invincible. They were gods. They believed they would never hurt, suffer or splatter.

Miles kept checking the power lines, hoping to catch a glimpse of the owl. But it was gone like the sun. He was alone. Lonely for long summer days where he worked hard and didn't have the energy or time to consider his medication. He took it with food and when he wasn't working he slept, too tired to remember his dreams, his lungs full of salt air.

He noticed Bikini Beach was coming up on the left. The parking lot was filling up and at the centre of each of the cartoon tits were blinking red lights and the cab seemed to be slowing down. Miles looked at the driver through the rearview. His teeth were like a saw blade. They were white next to raw gums.

"I just want to go home," Miles pleaded, and he knew the cab was about to turn into the parking lot so he opened the door. He jumped out, surprised at just how fast they were moving. He tumbled. He hurt. He was flying. He was free.

13

People were gathered in a group by the casket with their backs to the wind and snow. Mum was one of them. She held her yellow hair out of her face and cried black tears. Grampy put his arm around her. I walked away from them, past graves that were so old they seemed burnt. I couldn't read them. I doubted anybody could, even my teacher, and I climbed a hill. At the top the wind was strong and I could see the ocean. It was dark. The sky was grey. Miles was dead. But he was still my cousin. Just because everybody else got sad and gave up on him didn't mean I had to. I didn't want him ending up like the others. Boxed and buried. Burnt black and forgotten.

"Travis, we're going," Mum yelled.

I turned and the wind blew me down the hill. At the bottom I tried to stop in front of them but I slid on the snowy grass like a surfer and into Grampy. It felt like I hit a wall even though he was old.

"Jesus," said Mum.

"Start the car, he'll follow," he said to Mum, and he put one of his hands on my shoulder. Ever since I can remember I've been afraid of those hands. They're big and blue-veined and I once saw them punch through a barn wall.

Mum walked ahead. "Sorry," I said to Grampy.

"It's not about that," he said. "Your mom needs a man around right now, not a boy. Follow?" he said, brushing away the snowflakes that were melting on the bald top of his head. He had bushy grey eyebrows and red eyes.

"No," I said.

"I need you to start acting like a man."

"I'll try."

"You want to do more than try or I'll have you come stay with me. I'll teach you real quick how to be a man," and he squeezed my shoulder. My body shivered with pain and he let go.

"Does this mean I have to quit school and get a job?" I said.

"No," he said, shaking his head. "I just mean you have to act mature. Make life easy on your mum."

"I always do that now that dad is in jail. I rub her feet almost every night," I said, and I held up my hands. They weren't as big or blue-veined as Grampy's but with a little more rubbing and growing they could be.

"Good," Grampy said, and looked past me and nodded at a man who was leaning on a shovel next to a mound of snow-covered dirt. "Now go with your Mum. I got something to take care of here."

We drove along country roads. They were snow covered with tire tracks. The wipers cleaned the windshield. With my eyes I searched the ditches and fields and between trees while Mum sniffled. She wore a long black coat and beneath that a black dress.

"Why was everybody wearing black?" I said.

"It's the colour that people wear when they're grieving," she said.

"What's grieving?"

"It's when you're sad about somebody dying."

"Why aren't I wearing black then?"

"You don't own anything black."

"My black underwear."

"Shut up. Just shut up unless you have something important to say," Mum said, and she squeezed the wheel so hard that her knuckles turned white.

"Do men get Christmas presents?"

"Of course they do."

"Good. When are you going to get my Christmas present?"

Her eyes went from the road to me and back to the road. They blinked. "Tomorrow's Christmas," she said, and one black tear fell slowly down her cheek, leaving a line. Her face was a bunch of black lines and with the black coat she looked like a girl who sang loud music on the TV. Not my mum.

The peeing church was halfway between Grampy's and town. Some of its white paint was falling off and next to it was a graveyard and I didn't have to pee until I saw its pointy top. The whole time I stood over the toilet with the crooked seat I thought of Miles. How one time at this spot we peed into the bowl at the same time, racing to see who could get all the yellow pee out first. Miles was older than me and he won.

When I got back in the car I said to Mum, "Are you still deciding?"

"Deciding? With your cousin, and your dad going off to jail."

"But you said men get Christmas presents. And I'm a man."

"A real man should understand he doesn't always get what he wants."

"But I'm not a real man. I just became one so I'll be learning for a while."

"Not this year."

I thought about it for a second. "But this could be my last year," I said. "Next year I could fall and hit my head."

More black tears. She blinked. She cleaned her eyes with the back of her hand.

"Have you decided yet?" I said.

She said something, but I didn't hear her. "What?" I said.

"Now," she said. "I'm going to get your present now, but stop fucking staring at me. You're always staring."

So I looked straight ahead. There were now more cars and less snow on the pavement and we were no longer in the country. I could see the Charlottetown Mall in the distance. It had a lot of stores. My favorite one had plastic bugs and puke and cushions that farted. It was fun to play with that stuff but I never asked Mum to buy me any of it because where I lived bugs and puke and farts were free. Trips to McDonald's weren't.

Mum found a spot at the back of the parking lot. She looked at her face in the mirror. "I'm a wreck," she said, and she licked her fingers and wiped the black lines until they were gone. She stuck out her lips like she was going to kiss the mirror. She rubbed them with lipstick.

"What do you want?" she said.

I smiled. "McDonald's Playland," I said. "But not the one at McDonald's, we don't have room for it. I want the one in the box that I saw on the TV."

"What if they're sold out?"

"Then I want a cat."

"You're not getting a cat."

"How about a fish?"

"No, you'll kill it."

"I want a black outfit then. For grieving."

She shook her head and said, "Wait in the car. I'll try not to be long."

"Can I go with you?"

"No, it'll be a zoo."

"I like zoos. Calgary has a zoo. Miles went there once and saw bears and marching penguins."

The door slammed and Mum disappeared behind a van. I watched snow collect on the windshield and thought about Playland. How after fifteen minutes of climbing and sliding and swimming in balls Mum would stand and cross her arms and tell me we're going. I never in my life got enough of Playland, not even the time Dad forgot me there all afternoon, but I hoped that would soon change.

I was excited but also afraid they wouldn't have any so I searched for something to take my mind off my Christmas present. Between the seats I found a scraper. I tried to clean the windows with it but all the snow was on the outside. I opened the drawer in front of me. It was empty except for a book about the car and a set of glasses. The glasses were big and gold and I tried them on. My world went blurry. I stared into the mirror and it was strange but I looked like Grampy, minus the wrinkles and plus a few teeth. It was fun looking like him, even if the glasses stung my eyes, because he was old and tough and I decided I would try being him. It would pass the time, plus it would give me practice at being a man for Mum.

I climbed into the driver's seat. I rolled down the window and hung my arm outside because Grampy drove like that, even in the winter. He chewed the insides of cigarettes too. But I couldn't find any so I chewed a mustard-stained napkin that I found on the floor and watched the parking lot. Cars came and went. So did people and when any of them got close enough to the car I nodded my head at them and said in my deep Grampy voice, "Afternoon." One man stopped and stared. His ponytail flapped in the wind like a flag.

"It's rude to stare," I said.

"Sorry," he said, and he rubbed his eyes. "How old are you?"

I told him Grampy's age and he said, "I didn't ask how old your glasses are." I told him Grampy's age again.

"You're a saucy thing."

"What's a saucy thing?"

"Look in the mirror and you'll see one."

I did and I laughed. I saw me.

"Want some company?"

I thought about it and decided that Grampy liked the company of other men, especially if they could talk about cars or chickens or weather or woodpiles.

"Okay," I said.

The man walked around to the passenger's side. He opened the door and got inside.

"Some car, eh?" I said.

"Sure," said the man.

"It has a motor."

"I know."

"Yes sir," and I spit the gob of napkin out the window because it was hard to talk with it in my mouth. "A big motor," I said.

"Okay, I get it," said the man. "Enough with the act," and he grabbed Grampy's glasses from my face. He set them in the cup holder and with my world un-blurred I noticed his ketchup-red hair, fuzzy cheeks and long pointy nose.

"You look like a fox," I said.

"That's original," he said.

"Thanks," I said, glad I was no longer Grampy because I knew he would never make nice with a man who looked like a fox, even if that man walked on two legs and wore a winter coat and had ponytail instead of a regular tail that was bushy and hid its bum.

"Seriously, how old are you?"

I told him. But I also told him that today I became a man. That I had to. For Mum.

"And where's your mum?"

"In the mall."

"Has she been gone long?"

"No, but it feels long."

"They're lined up in there."

"Do you know McDonald's Playland?"

"Sure."

I told him how right now Mum was trying to buy me one in a box. I told him how never in my life I got enough Playland but I hoped that would soon change.

"You can never have too much Playland," he said.

We both smiled.

"I see something shiny in your ear," he said. "Mind if I grab it?"

"No," I said.

He reached out and touched my ear. His fingers were gentle and it felt like a Dandy longlegs was exploring the folds. My whole body shivered.

"There, I got it," he said, and his hand pulled away from my ear. In it was a loonie. "It's yours," he said.

I took it. It looked real and I made it disappear because it was one thing to make nice with a man fox but it was another to trust him with your chickens. I learned that from Grampy. He was at war with the foxes that lived around his place. He would set traps and come after them with his shotgun. He even dropped beer bottles full of fire down into their dens. But it didn't matter what he did, every year they ate as many of his chickens as he did. And out where Grampy lived chickens were better than paper money. Country gold, he called them.

I felt something else in there, the man said. I think it was a five-dollar bill, but in order to get it I'll have to come closer, dig a little deeper.

I stuck my hand in my ear but couldn't feel any money. I knew there was enough fox in him that I probably couldn't trust him but five bucks plus the loonie in my pocket was two Happy Meals at McDonald's, two trips to Playland, so I told him okay.

He leaned in. He licked his fingers like they were covered in chicken grease and squished them into my ear. This time he went deeper, and it felt like he was making a den in there or something.

"I almost got it," he said. "Don't worry," he said, and while his hand dug around my ear he moaned and I tried to forget what was going on by looking out my side window. I saw swirls of snow, shopping carts and between two cars I saw my cousin Miles. His head was shaved. There was a scar where the doctors had cut him open. His skin was the colour of bone. He stared at me for a few seconds, as long as it took me to wave, and then disappeared.

"Miles," I yelled.

"What?" said the man, his finger leaving my ear.

"I just saw my cousin Miles".

"Where?"

I pointed.

"He's gone?"

"He'll be back. I know it."

The man's mouth fell open like a mailbox. His face went as red as his hair. He was all fox now and I saw the bill in his hand.

"You found five bucks," I said.

He didn't answer me. He didn't even seem to hear me. He opened the door and ran off with my money and I was surprised but I knew I shouldn't be. He was all fox, that one. His clothes and ponytail were a disguise.

I kept a lookout for Miles in case he reappeared. He didn't, and I was sad for the first time that day because I was so close to having my cousin back and finding five more bucks but now he was gone and so was the money.

I was sad right up until I saw Mum carrying a big frown on her face and a big bag in her hand. "I'm not wrapping it," she said. "So there you go."

I climbed into the backseat and looked in the bag. "Playland," I said, and I started to open it.

"Christ. Not until we get home."

Yesterday I would've cried until she let me open it. Not today. Today I was a man and men have money in their pockets and don't cry over toys or when somebody takes something from them they never even knew they had. I told Mum I was okay with that.

"Who are you?" she said. "And what did you do with Travis?"

I didn't have an answer for her right away. On the drive home I thought about the answer I owed her, and about Playland and Miles too, and when she parked Grampy's car outside of our apartment building I told her I left the old Travis back at the graveyard. "He's boxed and buried," I said. "Burnt black and forgotten."

14

"Let's go," Mum said when I walked into the kitchen.

Jody was sitting in a chair next to the table. Mum was sitting on his lap wearing a long black coat and dress and these things on her legs that looked like black spider webs. Jody was rubbing the webs nice and slow and the last time I saw Mum in that dress was over a year ago at Miles' funeral. That was back when Mum didn't know Jody and I had her all to myself.

I would've stopped and gave the webs a rub too but I was busy. I checked the chair in the living room again and under all the beds. I rechecked the closets and the basement. I even crawled under the deck in case he was there digging for worms but Miles was nowhere. I wanted to invite him to my thirteenth birthday party at McDonald's but it was beginning to look like he went out west again without saying goodbye. It was April and I hadn't seen him for almost three months, since he knocked on my door. He had been tired from all his digging and walking and I led him into the chair in the living room. One second I was watching him sleep, the next I had forgotten everything I ever knew, including who I was and what I loved (Mum and Miles and Happy Meals) and didn't love (Jody and Dad and

Jody). When I woke up in the morning the chair was empty and I still didn't know who I was. It took me almost the whole day to remember everything, which was how Miles had said it felt to die. With a bunch of grunts he had said it was like a deep sudden forgetting mixed with a dark sudden sleep. When I realized Miles was gone again I wasn't sad because I was busy feeling lucky. Nobody had time to box and bury me since I was only dead for a night.

When I crawled out from under the deck Mum was standing there with her arms crossed.

"You're filthy," she said.

I looked down at my clothes. Mum was right.

"You can clean up there," she said. "Come on."

Jody drove. Mum was in the front seat next to him. I was in the backseat with my birthday present. It was wrapped in a Zeller's flyer and I couldn't take my eyes off it.

"Can I open it?" I said.

"No," Mum told me, "not until we got to McDonald's." But then she changed her mind and said, "Actually, you could use it. Open it if you want."

I ripped it open and found a black sweatshirt and black gym pants.

"You remembered," I said.

Mum nodded.

"And when I'm not grieving it will be my spying outfit."

"There you go," said Mum.

"Jesus," said Jody.

"What?" said Mum.

"You know he's delusional. Why encourage him?"

"What you call delusions I call imagination," she said. "Besides, it's his day. Let him imagine what he wants or don't come with us. I told you what happened last year. He deserves a good day."

Jody kept his eyes on the road, chewing his lip like it was a stick of gum. Mum sighed and looked out the window. I thought about my last birthday. How Mum forgot it, and when I reminded her she put on a puffy white marshmallow of a coat and took a taxi to get me a present and when she got home a day and a half later her coat was gone and she was shivering and had bruises on her wrists and sour breath and twelve donuts in a box.

"Happy Birthday," she said. She went and locked herself in the bathroom and either cried or laughed in there, I couldn't tell which. The donuts were hard like old dog poop but they tasted good, especially the ones with filling, and I ate six of them as fast as I could and that was the worst birthday of my life but still it ended up better than a lot of days because even if the donuts came late the only reason I got them was because of my birthday.

Jody pulled up in front of the door to McDonald's.

"So what?" Mum said. "You really aren't coming?"

"I'm in no mood to pretend."

"Christ. I was in no mood to wear fishnets but look at my legs. They're uncomfortable and cold but I got them on. I wore them for you."

"What do you want me to say?"

"Travis, wait for me outside," Mum said.

Holding my present I got out of the car. I could already smell the Happy Meals and my belly was grumbling at me, telling me how hungry it was, and I watched Mum and Jody through the car window. They were stretching their lips, their faces full of colour. Then Mum put her feet on the dash and reached up under her skirt and took off her black spider webs. She got out of the car and held up the webs for Jody to see before throwing them in the garbage.

"Never again," Mum yelled.

Jody screeched off and I was happy that he was gone because I'd rather go to McDonald's with a pack of hungry coyotes than him. Mum looked sad though. Then she said, "If you dress like a slut, they'll treat you like one."

I told Mum she was the prettiest slut in town but that didn't seem to cheer her up.

Grampy was sitting by a table near the door. He stood when we came in. I looked past him at the ladders and tunnels and slides in Playland. I was excited for all the fun I was going to have after I ate.

Mum touched my shoulder and said, "Grampy's talking to you."

When I looked at Grampy I only saw the big brown buckets of skin beneath his eyes. They came after Miles died. When I asked Mum about them she told me he was having trouble sleeping. That we all have our scars, it's just that some of us do a better job of hiding them.

"Happy Birthday," Grampy said. He shook my hand. He pressed something into it and when I pulled my hand away there was twenty bucks inside. Last year he gave me five bucks for my birthday. I felt rich.

"That's a lot of money," Mum said.

"He's all I got," Grampy said.

"I know why you're doing this."

"So let me do it."

"Travis, tell Grampy thank you and then go get changed."

I brought my presents into a bathroom stall with me. I wasn't grieving but I planned on doing some spying in Playland. When I was putting on my new black outfit I heard the bathroom door open. Boots scraped across the floor. I held my breath and stood as still as a spy. They stopped outside my stall. They were black and covered in fresh red mud. The same boots that almost got me sent to the nuthouse when they made a mess of Jody's white kitchen floor.

"What took you so long?" Mum said.

"Birthdays are full of surprises," I said, and I was so hungry I ate like my neighbour Winston's pet pig. I snorted and swallowed food before I even had time to chew it. When I wasn't snorting I heard parts of Mum and Grampy's conversation. Mum didn't like that Grampy was living out in the country all by himself.

"You're a hermit," she said. "We never see you."

Grampy didn't like Jody one bit and said, "The way he looks at you, the way he talks to you. I don't know, he just doesn't have any respect. After what happened to your sister and Miles, I don't think we should ever settle. Life's too short for that."

"Miles is here," I said when I finished my last fry.

"Don't start," Mum said.

"You can stop wearing your grieving outfit," I said to Mum. "And Grampy, your scars will go away."

"Travis," Mum said.

"Miles is alive. I left him in the bathroom. I wanted him to come out but he wouldn't. He doesn't like sunlight anymore and he's shy."

"Jesus Christ!" Mum said.

"I'll go see if he's changed his mind."

Grampy caught up to me before I could open the bathroom door. I felt his strong hand on my shoulder and he turned me around. He told me to explain myself. So I told him about Miles knocking on my door. How he grunted and only ate worms. How death was lonely without a friend and that was why he came back.

Grampy then told me how he saw Miles after he died too. Only once. They walked along the beach and through the path in the trees that led to the graveyard. There was no talking. Just the crunch of their footsteps in the snow and the cold wind and the sound of the waves followed them into the trees. They both knew what was coming, but they were happy to have each other close. They stopped and stared at an old maple. It was naked except for the lichens. When they got to the graveyard there was a pile of dirt. Next to it a hole in the ground.

"Our walk was our goodbye," Grampy said, shaking, bringing me in close and hugging me tightly like I was his pillow.

I noticed that Grampy had changed after Miles died. It wasn't just the scars. He lost the something inside of him that made him tough. And he was nicer. I had twenty bucks in my sock to prove it.

"What I'm trying to say is that not everything we experience is real," Grampy said. "It might've felt real when I saw him in my dream, but he's gone."

Grampy let go of me and I opened the bathroom door. I searched in the stall. My yellow pee was still on the toilet seat but there was no Miles.

"I'm sorry," Grampy said.

I was sorry too until I came out from the stall and saw mud on the floor where I first saw Miles' boots. That told me all I needed to know.

We went back to Mum and I ate my cookies and finished my orange drink. Then I went to Playland where I climbed and crawled and slid and spied on Mum and Grampy from my hiding place under the slide. They didn't believe me. That was Miles' fault because he was always disappearing. I didn't know where to. But I figured he went underground with the worms that he ate. All I knew for sure was that I was angry. It was the only thirteenth birthday I'd ever have and I saw him for just minutes in the bathroom. I didn't care if he didn't like sunlight and was shy. I wanted my cousin back. Not some dumb grunting worm eater.

15

I opened my eyes. I saw dusty sunlight and I was so excited for the day that I screamed and pounded the bed with my fists until my door flew open. It was Mum. She had sleep lines on her face and she said, "What? What?"

"It's the first day of summer vacation," I said.

She wiped her eyes and gave me a look.

"You can call my teacher if you don't believe me."

"I believe you. Christ. I just don't believe that you woke me up at five in the morning with your antics."

"What are antics?"

She shook her head.

"Everything you do is an antic. One goddamned antic after another and you wanna know what? I'm getting tired of it."

She slammed my door. She slammed her door next and I got dressed, glad that she was gone because there was another reason I was excited for today. One I didn't share with Mum because any time I ever talked about Miles coming back to life she cursed at me like a rapper and raised her hand like she was about to hit me but I knew she would never. She was all bark, Dad used to say.

I walked down the hall and into the living room and stopped in front of the chair. Miles was still sleeping. He was wearing the same clothes he was buried in, a white sweater and blue pants that were now a muddy brown from all the time he had spent underground with the worms so that the only reason I even knew the sweater was supposed to be white was because I went to the wake and funeral.

I was about to wish him a good morning when I thought of an even better way of waking him. By delivering him breakfast in bed. Or in his case breakfast in chair, and I smiled because I wanted this to be our best day ever. Even better than the one we spent with our mums at the beach, swimming and splattering jellyfish that washed up onto shore by dropping big heavy rocks on their heads.

I crawled through the shadows under the deck. I couldn't see much so I felt with one hand while I dug with the other. Finally I felt a worm and it squirmed and I put it in my coat pocket. I found one more but there weren't many around and so I searched a few more spots around the street, like Winston's pig pen (he ate last year's pig but there was a new one there now) and Georgina's garden but when I emptied my pocket onto a plate in the kitchen I counted only three worms. They looked more like a snack so I squirted two gobs of ketchup onto the plate to make it a meal. I walked out to the living room, holding the plate in front of my face like Mum did when she delivered food at the restaurant. But the chair was empty. Miles was gone. And lying on the couch watching TV was Jody.

"What?" he said.

"Miles," I said.

"What about Miles?"

"He's gone."

"How many times do we have to tell you? He's been gone a long time."

"But he came back."

"No, he didn't."

"He was just sleeping right there. "

I pointed. Jody looked over at the chair and sighed.

"They really gotta up your dosage," he said.

I pretended I didn't hear him. He was always going on about upping the dosage of my medication. Saying it will straighten me out as if I was bent like a spoon or something and I walked over to the chair and looked behind it.

"Those are worms," he said.

"I didn't say anything."

"On a plate, like you're about to eat them."

I was too busy searching for Miles to explain and the next thing I knew he was yelling for Mum. She came running wearing a purple bra and black panties and as soon as she was in the room he started yelling at her about worms and medication.

When he finished Mum said, "I gotta be at work in twenty minutes. It could've waited."

"The kid's about to dine on worms and you think it could've waited?"

Mum looked from Jody to my plate.

They started yelling at each other about whether or not I was going to eat the worms. So I set them on the chair and searched every dark place in the house for Miles, even the hole in the wall in the basement where Jody used to keep his pictures of naked girls. There was no sign of Miles or the pictures, so I decided to go and check the chair one last time for any clues.

Jody was still lying on the couch but the worms were gone. I looked under the seat cushion in case Miles left a note there. All I found were chip crumbs and a dime. After I put the money in my pocket Jody turned the volume down on the TV and said, "You just missed him."

I turned around.

Jody smiled. "Yeah, he went to McDonald's," he said. "He said something about getting a Happy Meal."

"But he doesn't even eat McDonald's anymore," I said.

Jody shook his head and said, "That's not what he just told me. He said that he's sick of worms. Actually, he said that he's sick of a lot of things. Mainly your antics. That's why he went to McDonald's."

"Did he say when he was gonna be back?"

Jody didn't answer me. He smiled and turned the volume back up on the TV and began searching through the channels for something to watch. There was sad music and pictures of kids that Mum called the starving Africans. Their eyes were big and their bellies were round and I didn't know how they could be starving when their bellies were so big. Jody changed the channel. Now there was a woman holding toothpaste, talking about how white it made teeth and I thought Miles could use a good tooth brushing. His mouth was the colour of poop.

Since everything I wanted to do today was with Miles, I decided I would wait for him to get home. I knew just the spot to do my waiting. Before I went outside I loaded my pockets with cereal. It tasted like Styrofoam but it filled my belly.

It was warm in the sun and I went straight to my spot below the living room window. All of the bushes at the front of the house had roses and thorns except the one I hid behind. It blocked the sun but I could see through the leaves and I watched the people on my street do stuff like mow their lawns or scratch their bum holes but they couldn't see me and what I was up to in the bushes.

For the first half of the day I was sad. Because Miles went to McDonald's without me. But also because he didn't like my antics, and on top of that we were missing out on a chance to do some fun things, like smash pop bottles, squash earwigs, and feed Mr. Winston's new pet pig. I hoped it was just like the old one, who would eat anything, onionskins, even used toilet paper. It would gobble it all down and then start snorting for more like it was just fed turkey dinner or something.

But for the second half of the day, the part where the sun got covered by the clouds and my neighbour Michelle with the big coconuts got up off her blanket and went inside, I was angry. I decided that I didn't like Miles' antics either. Ever since he came back to life all he did was eat, sleep, and disappear. One time he was gone for three months, other times he was gone for days and then I would find him sitting on a bench in the mall or standing next to a slide outside my school with the wind blowing his clothes and then it would be a few more weeks before I would find him in the chair again, grunting, and when I'd ask him where he was he would just go on grunting for worms and let me tell you, digging for them was dirty hard work. And when I would finally have a couple to offer him, he would just stuff them into his mouth and chew, and they wouldn't even be gone, there'd be squirming bits of worm still stuck to his teeth, when he'd be grunting for more. He always wanted more like a pig but then he gave nothing. Not even a happy smile and I thought about what Grampy told me.

"If a cow can't give you any milk," he said, "she wasn't worth the feed. Send her to the slaughterhouse."

"What's a slaughterhouse?" I said.

"It can be any old place. A shed or a barn. Just as long as you got a cattle gun and a freezer."

"What's a cattle gun?"

He tapped me between my eyes.

"Hold it there, pull the trigger, and in a blink the cow is dead."
He spit.
I blinked.
"There you go, one dead cow."
I blinked again.
"Two."
And again.
"You're a greedy little man," he said. "Three."

It was fun. I blinked for weeks and imagined all the cows in all the fields from here to China dropping dead. And there being so much extra meat in the world that McDonald's had to cook it up and give away hamburgers for free to people like me and the starving Africans.

The wind started to blow. The bushes shook and the clouds slid so that I could see the sun again. It was low in the sky. Red and shining like a dot of blood and I wished that that was Miles' blood. That he was dead again and my life was back to normal. None of this waiting and wondering and only coming to my birthday for five minutes. None of this wasting my winters and springs and first days of summer vacation.

A dog barked.

I snacked on Styrofoam.

Mum got home from work.

I rubbed my bird and closed my eyes. I did some thinking and even a little sleeping and when I opened them the sky was dark. Most of the houses were dark too and I hoped that Miles was inside.

In the kitchen I turned on the light. There was a pill and a glass of water on the table. I grabbed a steak knife and left the pill and when I got to the living room my mind wasn't so made up anymore.

Miles was back sitting in the chair, sleeping. Because of a shadow I couldn't see his scar or bone-coloured skin or even a single speck of dirt on his face or clothes. He almost looked like the old Miles who starred in all the good memories in my mind.

I lifted my knife, telling myself that it was a cattle gun. That this was the slaughterhouse. That the old Miles was gone and in his place a cow.

I blinked and he was dead.

16

I had to bury him. Jody gave me no choice. He was back from flying planes tomorrow and before he left he said that if my bed blanket wasn't gone from the chair when he got home he'd burn it. That would be bad because he'd discover what was under it and then I would go to jail. And I didn't want to go to jail because Dad's friend Boomer called it the holding tank, and the only holding tank I knew was at the grocery store and it was filled with rusty lobsters. Their claws were clamped and they were tangled like spaghetti and I wanted no part of that.

I wished I still had the shovel Grampy gave me for an old birthday. I remembered how before I even opened any other presents I ran outside and dug and buried anything I could find. The next morning Dad was searching for his wallet and he asked me if I saw it. I told him I saw it right before I buried it. Dad said fuck. We never did find his wallet and my shovel also disappeared.

The first person I thought of who had a shovel I could borrow, besides Grampy who lived out in the country, was Georgina. She was our neighbour and lived in a house like ours, only it was surrounded by a giant garden. It was as colourful as a rainbow. It smelled as good as the perfume Jody gave Mum for Christmas. And it was home to all sorts of bugs and birds.

Georgina got paid to work in her garden. I knew this because she was friends with Mum and when they got together on our deck I would put on my spying outfit and crawl underneath and listen. Lying with the slugs and the worms I learned that Georgina's favourite thing to do was talk in her angry voice about her ex-husband. She told Mum that he was always horny, and how he used to wake her in the night by poking his bird up inside of her. She said that that sort of horniness can't be satisfied by one woman alone, and how really it was no surprise he left her for someone known as the taxi.

"You pay, you get your rides," she said. "And he paid. Let me tell you, those rides cost him."

She talked about how when her husband left he gave her the house. He also started paying her to work in its garden, but for only as long as it took her to get another job or a new husband. Whatever came first.

"Fuck that, I say," and she flicked ashes from her cigarette over the side of the deck. "He'll be paying me until I croak. Because if I only accomplish one thing in this life, it will be to teach him a lesson. Seriously. Think with your wallet, not with your dick, asshole."

Mum made a sound with her mouth that was barely a laugh.

"How long since he left?"

She didn't answer right away. Another drag on her cigarette.

"Eleven years," she said.

"Oh," Mum said.

"I know, I know, you don't need to say it. It's all over your face," she said, getting up to leave. "I gotta turn on my sprinklers."

"Georgina, stay. Have another drink."

"I might've given up on myself, but not on my garden. Not yet anyway." And it was her turn to barely laugh.

I knocked on Georgina's door. There was no answer. I walked across the deck and around to the back of her house. Her yard smelled of just-cut grass and was empty except for sun and a bunch of flowers and this bee. It was buzzing mad for some reason and flying in crazy circles and when it saw me it decided to attack. I did this jumping kick that I saw on the TV. It was supposed to knock things out but I was still learning it and I missed the bee and fell. Lucky for me I landed on the grass and the bee didn't get me with its stinger.

I got back up and tried knocking on the door again. She still didn't answer and when I saw the time on the clock in her kitchen I knew why. It was soap time. I learned from my spying that she loved her soaps as much as Mum, and like Mum she got cozy and watched and I bet door knocking or even the phone couldn't get her up off the couch. I opened the door and went inside.

Her kitchen reminded me of her garden. Its walls were covered in pretty yellow paper with big red flowers. It smelled nice, like every window in the house was open and I thought I could smell popcorn.

A commercial was playing on the TV in the living room and the couch was empty except for a bed pillow and a bowl of popcorn. I was bent over it filling my mouth when I heard Georgina scream. I turned but she was already gone and I figured whatever she was afraid of, that angry bee maybe, I should be afraid of it too and I followed her out into the backyard where I saw her hide behind a bush.

"You can have whatever you want but stay back," she said.

I chewed and swallowed the popcorn in my mouth. I was thirsty after that and I said, "What about McDonald's Orange Drink?"

"What?" she said.

"It tastes like pop but it's smooth like juice."

She stuck her head out. "Travis," she said, blocking the sun from her eyes.

"Yeah," I said.

She walked out from behind the bush and said, "You scared the hell out of me. Jesus, didn't anybody ever teach you to knock?"

"Yeah."

"Well?"

I didn't know what to say so I stayed quiet and stared. Georgina was short and thin and her skin was the colour of plastic-wrapped caramels. She wore a robe that was untied. My eyes went down to her coconuts, only they weren't like the coconuts I was used to seeing in Jody's pictures.

"At least somebody's getting some enjoyment out of them," she said. "Seriously, he never appreciated them."

I wanted to tell her that I wasn't enjoying looking at them. That they were shriveled like unpicked mushrooms dying in our yard, but before I got a chance to say anything she covered them with her robe and said, "You really came looking for some sort of orange drink?"

"No, I came to borrow your shovel," I said.

"What do you need a shovel for?"

I didn't know what to tell her. I looked around her garden. Sweat fell from the corner of my nose and landed in my mouth.

"I need to bury my pet parrot," I said.

"I didn't know you had a parrot," she said.

"I do."

"You mean you did?"

"Yeah."

"How'd your parrot die?"

Since she thought I was talking about our parrot I decided to go with the truth and said, "I slaughtered him."

Her face wrinkled and she stared, but I was used to that stare, the trying to figure me out, because ever since I can remember I was a puzzle to people. There was a time when I didn't know what to think of it, but now I expected it, even liked it because it was one of the things I was best at. That and spying and sleeping and eating McDonald's. One day I hoped to add jump kicking to that list.

"And why'd you slaughter him?" she said.

"He fell and hit his head," I said. "He was never the same after that."

"Tell me your mother knows what happened."

"She does, but I don't want her to see him like that."

"You wouldn't have met Lily. My cat. It was before you guys moved in. One day she stopped eating. She would just lay on her side and cry and the only time she wasn't crying was when she was sleeping. It near drove me crazy. But I don't trust vets. They charge you a load just to look over them and then they say what you could tell just by looking in their eyes. I went out back, dug a hole right over there, laid her inside, and it wasn't pretty but I sent her to a better place."

"I used to have a cat," I told her, "but no matter how much I rubbed its belly I could never get it to purr."

"Oh, Lily purred alright. She used to sleep beside me and would wake me in the night with her purring," she said, trying to smile through the tears that were filling her eyes.

I knew what it was like to miss somebody who died and I walked up to her and hugged her. She smelled of shampoo and she was cozy like my bed blanket and even though I didn't like her mushrooms my bird got tingly and grew. Soon our birds were touching through our clothes and I bet I reminded her of her husband, the bird poker, because she hugged me even tighter and moaned. My dizziness came on like a sneeze and one second my bird was full of white pee, the gooey kind that felt good when it came out, and the next second my underwear were soaking wet and my knees wobbled but she held me up. I stayed in her special hug until she trembled and pushed me away.

"I'm missing my show," she said, her face puffy and red and she looked like a sunburnt caramel.

I was really thirsty now and I said, "After your show do you want to go get some McDonald's Orange Drink?"

"Not today."

"Tomorrow?"

"We'll see. The shovel's in the shed."

I got the shovel and got out of her yard as quick as I could because it was hot in the sun and I knew that bee would be back. I went home and filled a glass with cold water from the kitchen sink. It got rid of my thirst but it was no McDonald's Orange Drink.

I yawned. I decided to sleep now and to go back out and dig when it was cool and dark. I got into bed. I reached for my blanket out of habit but all I got was thin sheet. I thought about how I couldn't wait to get my blanket back. Not just because I missed its coziness. With it I would finally be able to have the sleepover I'd been wanting to have all summer.

I was such a good sleeper I fell right to sleep. The next thing I knew I was swimming in a sea of McDonald's Orange Drink.

I splashed, did somersaults, swallowed mouthfuls of the orange stuff whenever I was thirsty. When the sun got too hot on my head I swam out deep and dived and pretended I was a fish. I didn't know what else fish did besides swim and swallow smaller fish, so that's what I did for as long as I could hold my breath. One of the times I came up for air I heard a voice.

"Get up," it said. I burped from all the drink and fish and looked around. I was alone except for Georgina, who was lying topless on the beach and rubbing the belly of a cat. I knew it was Lily from how happily she was purring. And Georgina's mushrooms weren't shriveled anymore, they were giant coconuts. I heard the voice again.

This time it said "Help me clean the house. Jody's coming home tomorrow."

At first I was confused, and then I realized it was Mum. But I wanted to get back to my dream, which was why I kept my eyes closed. She shook me, she even pinched my arm, but I pretended I was in a deep sleep. After a while she left me alone. Soon I was swimming back to shore to give Lily a pat and get another one of Georgina's special hugs. Soon I opened my eyes to a dark room. I wiped the crumbs from them and looked around. I knew it was the middle of the night because it was dark and I couldn't hear the TV.

I stood in front of the chair in the living room. I stared at the dark lump, afraid that he would feel mushy like a mushroom or hard like a coconut. I leaned in and lifted him over my shoulder. He wasn't as heavy as I thought he would be. He was bendy and soft without being mushy and he shaped to my body like a winter coat. I carried him out to the kitchen. I put on my shoes. I reached for the door. That was when I noticed the chimes. Mum started hanging them from the front and back door after the fire at Ada's. They were there to keep me in the house at night. I knew this because the last time I tried to sneak outside they chimed and Mum woke. She caught me on the deck and asked me what I was doing. I told her I was going to the field to listen to the crickets. She called me a liar and grounded me for a week. But what I told her was the truth. The cricket song was one of my favourites because of its pretty sound but also because of what Grammy told me about it. She said it was the song crickets sang when they made their babies. She called it the song of life. It was one of her favourite things before she went deaf and died.

I decided to go out my bedroom window. I knew it was too high for me to climb back in so I'd need to spend the rest of the night outside and hope Mum didn't come looking for me before I had a chance to sneak back in in the morning. At least I'd have my bed blanket to keep me cozy, I thought.

I closed my bedroom door and opened my window. I pushed him outside. The blanket unraveled in the air and he landed without a sound. It still hid most of him except for his boots and a small patch of skin that was white like the moon and I couldn't help but be sad even though I knew he was just a lump of skin and bones and clothes and hair and nothing more. The Miles I loved was gone, all that was left of him was dead meat.

I climbed out the window and hung from the ledge. I dropped to the grass and covered the rest of his face. Tears filled my eyes. The crickets made their babies. Wherever Miles went I hoped it was a better place like the one I visited in my dream where McDonald's Orange Drink was the new water and there was always sun and hugs and coconuts and Lily the purring cat.

17

Mum and Jody were fighting again. I heard them from my spot in the bushes below the living room window. Jody was angry that Mum was going to O'Leary for the weekend and leaving her crazy kid, me, behind. Mum was angry that Grampy's sister was dying and all Jody could think of was himself.

"He's hard enough on us and we're healthy," she said. "Dad's already on his way. I'm going. Deal with it."

"Yeah, I'll deal with it all right. I'll have me a good time dealing with it."

"I'm sure you will," she said, and the kitchen door slammed. I watched her carry her suitcase up the driveway. She wore a short white dress with a jean jacket over it. Her yellow hair was wet and shiny.

She dropped her suitcase when she got to the end of the driveway. She stuck her hand into her purse and came out with a cigarette and a purple lighter. I was surprised. I thought she quit. And worried too because I didn't want Mum catching fire and jumping through a window to try and escape it.

I wanted to warn Mum of the danger she was in and so I crawled out from the bushes and followed her up the driveway.

"Be careful with your smoking," I said. "Remember what happened to Ada."

She stared at me as she sucked on her cigarette.

I stared back.

But she still wasn't talking to me. The last time she talked to me was the morning Georgina woke her with a phone call. I bet it went something like this:

Georgina: "Do you know where your son is?"

Mum: "He better be in his room."

Georgina: "He isn't."

Mum: "Where is he?"

Georgina: "In my garden shed."

Mum: "I don't understand."

Georgina: "Don't understand what?"

Mum: "How he snuck past the chimes."

Georgina: "All I know is that my shovel's back and he's asleep in my shed."

Mum: "Where was your shovel?"

Georgina: "He borrowed it to bury your parrot."

Mum: "What parrot?"

Georgina told Mum all about our pet parrot and in seconds she was in Georgina's garden shed. She woke me with her yelling. Chimes this. Parrot that. She woke some of the neighbours too. They came to their windows or stood on their front steps in their pajamas and watched her haul me home. As soon as we got inside she stopped yelling. I thought that was a good thing until I told her I was hungry for breakfast and she stared at me, her answer was angry silence. And that was how she answered all my questions for what felt like forever, which turned out to be worse than grounding. Since Miles fell and hit his head, Mum was still my Mum but she was also my best friend.

Standing in our driveway, I wanted to say something to her that would get her talking to me again. I decided a message for Aunt Jean might do the trick. Some sort of love you and goodbye, and since I didn't know how to say goodbye to somebody who was dying, I decided to say what a nice old man with a crooked back once said to me when I was leaving his store.

"Will you give Aunt Jean a message for me?" I said.

Mum nodded.

"Tell her goodbye and good riddance," and I smiled probably the nicest smile of my life. It was all teeth.

Mum had just took a long suck on her cigarette, and as soon as I smiled a whole cloud of smoke burst from her mouth. At first I thought she was crying, but then I realized she was laughing like I hadn't seen her laugh in a long time.

"You're a piece of work, you know that?" she said.

I kept smiling.

"Does this mean you're talking to me again?" I said.

"I guess."

"Can I have a sleepover tonight?"

She rolled her eyes.

"With who?"

"I don't know, Georgina or Michelle. I didn't decide yet."

"Don't you think they're a little old for you?"

"No."

"And what exactly do you want to do on this sleepover?"

"Lots of things. Games and spying and special hugs."

"What do you mean by special hugs?"

I was about to say that I only ever had two of them, one was in a dream and the other was in a garden but they were both with Georgina and they had happy endings. But just as I started telling Mum about them Grampy's brown car showed up. She flicked her cigarette. It lay burning on the driveway.

"Let me guess, you didn't ask either one of them yet?" she said.

"No, not yet," I said.

"Well, sure, ask them, but I already know what they're gonna say."

"What? Tell me."

Mum just stared at me. "He's right, you know," she said. "I can't keep protecting you."

"Protecting me from what?"

Mum walked over to the car. She set her suitcase in the back and sat in the front. Grampy nodded at me. Mum rolled down her window.

"There's hotdogs in the fridge," she said.

When I could no longer see the brown car I jumped on the end of her burning cigarette and then brought it with me into the bushes. I did a lot of thinking and spying. I saw Winston walk down his driveway and root around the back of his truck until he pulled out a jam jar. His wife was at the picture window and with her sad hairy face she watched him drink it down. I saw kids with shiny bikes peddle past my house. They did pop-a-wheelies and laughed and I hoped all of them would get flat tires or fall and hit their heads. I saw some birds on a faraway power line. They weren't afraid of electricity but they now knew enough to stay away from me. I saw Jody go past the bushes. He carried the big black bag over his shoulder that he always brought with him when he was away flying planes. He walked up the street and disappeared around one of its snaky turns.

One of the things I thought about was who I wanted to have on my first ever sleepover. Georgina owed me a McDonald's Orange Drink and I was almost guaranteed one of her special hugs but I didn't like her mushrooms. Then there was Michelle, who was the prettiest girl I ever saw except for Mum. She had soft hair the colour of old pennies, cheeks as pink as her lips and big coconuts that I loved looking at but wondered if they would make it hard for me to get in close for a special hug.

I knew Mum said Dad was more full of shit than manure but it was something he told me that made me decide to visit Michelle first and ask her some questions. Always go for women with nice coconuts, he told me. That way when the bitch comes out, and she always does, at least you got something to look at.

From my spying I knew she had a doorbell. It wasn't everyday I got to ring one and from the front step I could hear it through the door. It sounded like the lonely church bell that played at

Miles' funeral. That was a sad day for everybody except for me. But if I knew then what I knew now it would've been a sad day for me too. I would've shook and snotted and sniffled and cried along with Mum in the cold church. I would've told him everything I didn't get a chance to tell him when he was alive. And when he was lowered into a hole in the ground I would've held Mum's hand and said goodbye.

When she opened the door I let go of the bell. Her hair looked even softer up close and she wore a leather vest that was too small to hide all of her coconuts, a short jean skirt that would make it easy for us to touch birds and shoes with heels as sharp as knives.

"What?" she said.

"I'm Travis," I said.

"I know. Is everything all right?"

I thought about it for a second. "Yeah," I said.

Jesus," she said. "With the way you were ringing the bell I thought something was wrong."

"Mum's talking to me again. I said goodbye to my cousin Miles. Nothing's wrong that I can think of."

"Are you looking for Jody?"

"No. I wouldn't go looking for him unless all the pilots in the world were dead and I needed him to fly a plane."

She scrunched her forehead and shook her head. "Anyway, what do you want?" she said.

"I have something I need to ask you."

"Make it quick. We're in the middle of something."

"Do you think your coconuts would make it hard for me to get in close for a special hug?"

"Coconuts?"

I pointed.

She slammed the door.

"Get your ass out here," I heard her yell.

When the door opened again I was surprised to see Jody's mean face.

"What?" he said.

"Mum said I could have a sleepover and I'm trying to decide who to ask."

Jody smiled. "Who's on the shortlist?" he said.

"Michelle and Georgina," I said.

"Tough call."

"I know."

"Hear that, Michelle. You should be flattered. You and Georgina made the kid's sleepover shortlist."

"You're a prick," she said. I couldn't see her but by the sound of her voice I knew she was close by.

"What's gonna go on at this sleepover?" he said.

"There's hotdogs in the fridge," I said. "And I want to have a special hug and now that I have my bed blanket back there will be lots of sleeping, too."

I thought I could hear Michelle laugh.

"So here are your options," Jody said.

"Don't waste my time," she said.

"No, no, you should always know your options in life. You can go with Travis here, eat some hotdogs, have a special hug and do a lot of sleeping. Or you can stay here with me, take more pictures, and if you aren't worn out after all of that maybe we can play our own little game of hide the hotdog."

I never heard of that game before, but hotdogs and hiding were some of my favourite things and I said, "Can you teach me the rules? I want to play it on my sleepover."

"Hear that?" Jody said. "Just when you thought the sleepover couldn't get any better."

"If you don't hurry up and get rid of him you'll be spending the night taking pictures of your own ass," she said, and by the sound her heels made when they stabbed the floor I knew she went to the other end of the house and Mum was right, I should never have listened to Dad. Nice coconuts don't make for nice people and I learned that the hard way.

"It isn't my fault she's not interested in your little sleepover," Jody said. "Go ask Georgina. She's so lonely she might even say yes."

"Why are you here?" I said.

"I don't answer to you. Soon it's going to be the other way around and I won't put up with your bullshit. Personally, I think you belong in some nuthouse. You're crazy. And if this summer is any indication, you're only getting worse."

"I'm not crazy," I said.

"Ada? Your blanket? That stuff isn't crazy?"

"Ada was an accident."

"Watching a woman burn and not doing anything about it. Some accident. And talking to your blanket, was that an accident, too?"

I didn't know what to say.

"Whole conversations with a fuckin blanket. That's crazy."

"Mum said that I'm not crazy, it's just that my mind is like a runaway train and I never know where it's going to take me."

"If your mum said that to you, then she's crazy. You're crazy. That dead cousin of yours was crazy. You know, it's like I'm marrying into the Addams Family, only crazier."

"Marrying?" I said.

"Your mum didn't tell you?"

"No."

"Big news. Supposedly we're getting married."

My head went hot like an oven cooking pizza. Suddenly I wanted to hurt Jody and I looked around for a weapon. The most dangerous one I could find was my foot and I jumped and kicked him in the belly. When I came down I landed on the outside of my foot and fell. My foot exploded with pain and I wanted to cry but I was too busy smiling. My kick was so good it could've been on the TV.

"You little nut," he said, bent over and holding his belly. "I've put up with a lot of your bullshit but those days are over."

He shut the door.

Soon the pain in my foot was replaced by a hot fuzzy feeling. I tried to stand but my foot wouldn't hold me up and I fell again. I crawled all the way home and when I passed Georgina's house I saw her working in her garden. I now knew who I wanted to have my sleepover with and I crawled down her ditch and across her lawn.

She looked up from her work and said, "Stop right there. Wherever you go, trouble follows," she said, and with her hands full of weeds she walked around to the back of her house.

Alone in her garden, I thought about what she said and knew she was right. Trouble did follow me and it used to be Dad but now its name was Jody. By the time I crawled into bed that night, six hotdogs hiding in my belly, I had decided something I should've decided a long time ago.

18

The phone rang. Jody was lying on the couch scratching his testicles and he jumped up to answer it. He was expecting a call. Ed from Toronto owed him money. Almost two grand for pictures he took of a tattooed skinny from Moncton, broke students from Fredericton and this real heifer from the Miramichi. He'd been calling Ed for the past month. Never an answer and not one returned call but then that happened in his line of work. A lot of pigs lying in their own shit. Pigs eating pork.

"Yeah," Jody said into the phone.

"Roses or lilies?" Trina said.

"What?"

"Me and the girls at work were talking. And we got it down to roses or lilies. For the wedding. What do you think?"

"Whatever."

She got quiet. In the background he heard clanking and talking. Food frying.

"What?" he said.

"Nothing," she said.

"Christ, Trina."

The phone clicked.

"Are you there?" he said, and when she didn't answer he slammed the phone in its cradle. It was Ed and the money, but it was also her. The kid. Their dramas. It was like they took turns. Today it was Trina and the flowers. The day before it was the kid and a crow. Through the living room window he had watched the kid sneak up behind one. Most kids entertained themselves by throwing baseballs at gloves. Not Travis. Yesterday he threw rocks at a crow until he wounded it. Then he kicked it around the yard as if it were a soccer ball, slowly torturing it. Finally, when there wasn't much life left in the animal, he jumped as high and far as he could and landed with both feet on its head. It was like he was a jock and death was his sport. Within minutes Jody found Travis standing in front of the open fridge, holding the bologna, trying to figure out how to unwrap it. It had come from Norman's. Jody had been saving it for Friday when he would roll his sleeves and fry it in bacon fat in the same cast iron pan his dad once used. But the kid already knew this. He had been told not to eat it. Jody's rage consumed him like a migraine. And afterwards it scared him to think of how he would've reacted if the kid had just a little more time to mangle the bologna as he did the crow.

The phone rang again. Jody rushed to answer it. He heard panting and traffic and he was almost certain it was Ed but of course it was Trina. She called him heartless. He asked where she was calling from.

"A pay phone outside the restaurant," she said. "It's not like I was gonna fight with you in front of the cooks."

"I hate to disappoint you," he said. "I'm not gonna fight."

"What's that supposed to mean?"

"With you everything has to mean something else."

"I'm a complex woman."

"And I'm looking to simplify my life."

"Just how do you plan on doing that?"

"Go back to work. It's not important," he said, not wanting to have this conversation now. Not without knowing if he was going to get his money from Ed.

"Jesus," she said.

"What?" he said.

"You're gonna call it off."

"I didn't say that."

"You didn't have to. Baby, I'm coming home."

He knew she was just seconds from hanging up and so he blurted it. "Roses," he said.

"What?" she said.

"I should've told you earlier. I think we should go with roses."

That bought Jody the rest of the afternoon. When he got off the phone with her he left another message for Ed, this time saying that if he didn't hear back from him by the end of the day he'd be paying a visit to Toronto.

"I'm not a violent man," he told Ed's machine. "But I'm desperate and there isn't a helluva lot of difference between the two."

The sun was white and glaring. The wind was up. It was the end of summer and already he could feel fall in the air. He walked to the end of the driveway and opened the mailbox. Nothing. As he walked back towards the house his eyes went to the field behind it. He noticed the kid. He could barely see his head above the wheat and he wondered what he was up to out there. It could've been nothing, but he doubted it.

The rest of the afternoon he went over bank statements, recorded Trina's soaps and left a few more messages for Ed. At the end of the last message he said the whole line about violence and desperation and only afterwards did he remember that he had already said it. He felt like a bad movie and after that performance he gave up hope of getting paid. Still he couldn't stop himself from glancing at the phone. Still he longed for it to ring. By the time evening came he found himself wishing it were true and that he was a pilot, that he got paid to fly far away from here.

Then Trina was home. She was showered, showing cleavage, but lately it was as if she had rocks for tits, they interested him that little. It hadn't always been like that.

"What's wrong?" she said.

"What makes you think something's wrong?" he said.

"The look on your face. How you were with me on the phone."

He had told her he was short on work but he didn't want to tell her about Ed and not getting paid because he knew whatever romantic nonsense she blurted, her message would be clear: if they stuck together they could get by on her income alone, for now anyway. What she didn't know was that staying together was his problem. Money, more than she made, the solution.

He said, which was hardly a lie, "Your kid, that's what's wrong."

"Are you still on about that crow?"

"Of course I'm still on about the crow. I watched him crush it like a pop can."

"They're rats with wings. As far as I'm concerned he's doing the world a favour."

"I'm telling you right now, the crows are only the beginning."

"I admit there's something wrong. We're trying him on medication. But he could be just at that age. He may grow out of it."

"I bet Mrs. Manson said something like that once. About her son, Charlie."

She laughed.

He couldn't help but laugh too even though he knew there was nothing funny about any of this.

The night was long like the day, the phone quiet, the kid nowhere to be found. They watched her soaps—he was now hooked on them, his excuse was that the fluff helped pass the time. They capped off the night with a bit of routine sex, sex that he salvaged by reaching around and shoving his finger up her butt. That got her moaning. She returned the favour. And in no time he was cumming, feeling as light as air and that nothing, nobody, could bring him down.

He rolled off of her. He lay naked, his back clinging to the satin sheets in the warm dark and he was just about asleep when she brought up the roses.

He didn't want to get into that right now and so he ignored her, but she grabbed his nipple and squeezed and there was no ignoring that.

"Jesus," he said.

"You weren't asleep yet," she said. "I could tell by your breathing."

"What do you want?"

"Roses aren't cheap."

"You better start taking on some extra shifts then."

"And what, you're just gonna sit around the house?"

"It's my goddamned house. I own it. So yeah, I am just going to sit around until some of my pictures sell."

"Well I can't pay for this wedding by myself."

"You should've thought about that before you asked me to get married."

"It's not like I asked you to go into business."

"Look, if you can't afford it, because I sure as hell can't, then we should hold off."

"No, no—".

He cut her off, saying, "We were drunk when you asked me. This will give us time to think about what we're doing. Lately, all we do is fight. Fight and screw."

"We do other things."

"Like what?"

"I don't know, we watch our soaps."

He laughed. "You can't be serious?" he said.

But she was serious. Jody told her how pathetic she sounded and they went at it into the morning. There was swearing, tears, a busted lamp and by the end of it he was ready to tell her to pack her things when he caught himself. He half remembered mumbling an apology so that she would leave him alone, let him sleep.

Jody got up around noon. Normally after a fight like that Trina would call in sick for work. Not today. She was already gone, probably hustling for tips to prove that they could afford a wedding.

Watching his coffee dribble, filling the pot he tried not to think about Trina or her kid or Ed. He was able to distract himself by thinking of Michelle. She knew how to manipulate men with her beauty and went through them like food. Jody was just happy to be on the menu. He also thought of the bologna, how he would fry it tonight in the bacon fat he had been saving in the freezer. Not that he had a long week of work to commemorate. More a long week to forget.

He checked the mailbox again, but the bills he found there only put him further in debt. He drank his coffee sitting on the step. The kid was back out in the field and he got this strange sinking feeling like his stomach was trying to come out his ass. Everything was exactly as it was yesterday, right down to the wind and the glare of the sun and he decided things had to change. Not with the whole porn business, he was still more than happy to get paid to take pictures of hard-hatted women bent over pallet jacks and the like. He meant with them, her and the kid. Just because he was stuck with them a while longer didn't meant he would have to keep tolerating their antics.

He finished his coffee.

The wind swirled and he was pushing through the field. Yesterday he left the kid alone. Today the kid was going to answer to him. And if he found a dead animal out there, as much as a mouse, he wouldn't be the only one the kid would be answering to. This was the sort of change he needed. This was only the beginning.

Jody came to an area where the wheat was pressed flat. The kid had just been there, he'd seen him from the step, but of course he was gone now. Probably hiding close by. Spying.

Jody noticed a patch of dirt in a clearing in the wheat. The dirt looked fresh enough. He noticed something sticking up from it. Two popsicle sticks were taped together to form what looked like a cross. There was writing on the sticks. He couldn't make it out but he knew whose it was.

Jody dropped to his knees and started digging. It wasn't long before he uncovered a shirt, jeans, boots and several cassettes, among them Bob Dylan. They had belonged to Miles. He knew this because for a few weeks this summer the kid had hid them under his blanket on the chair in the living room.

When Jody confronted Trina over this she said, "Look, he's no longer on about Miles coming back to life. I think he's finally accepted that he's gone. So if this is how he's gonna grieve, let him grieve is what I say. At least for a few more days anyway."

Holding a dead person's things, Jody almost felt guilty, there he was thinking the kid had murdered another small animal when all he had done was build a memorial for his dead cousin. Jody then thought of his parents. How it had been some time since he brought flowers to their graves.

He heard something coming through the wheat. He looked up. The kid was running at him, holding a good-sized rock. The kid reached the clearing and Jody quickly got over his surprise and found himself actually wanting to be hurt. Not badly, but enough that he had proof that the kid was a danger. That the medication wasn't enough. Instead of growing out of it, the kid was growing into it.

Jody brought his elbows up around his head as if he were blocking a punch. The kid threw the rock. Jody watched it fly through the air, braced for the pain of it hitting his arms but it flew past and got him in the nose. His head snapped back. He heard a bone break and almost instantly his nose was pouring blood. Stunned, he reached for the rock. The kid beat him to it and Jody tried to stand. He took another rock to the head and fell to the ground.

He could barely see for the blood in his eyes. Travis was a dark shape standing over him and Jody felt vindicated, knowing this would finally prove him right.

19

I wanted to play hide the hotdog and I went looking for Mum. I checked her bed, the couch and the kitchen table and I was starting to get worried when I found her out on the step. She was sitting there in her housecoat, sucking on a cigarette. There were two beer bottles between her legs. She tapped her cigarette into one of them and drank from the other.

"There you are," I said.

Mum kept on smoking and staring at the sky. It was the colour of wet newspaper. The wind was bending the trees. Summer was almost over and I didn't like that because when summer left so did the crickets and the heat and all the smelly flowers.

"Do you want to play hide the hotdog?" I said.

When Mum still didn't say anything I tugged on her arm.

"Jesus, what?" she said.

"I was talking to you," I said.

"Yeah, but I got nothing to say to you."

"Why?"

"Don't give me that shit. You know exactly why."

Mum dropped her smoke into one of the bottles as she stood up.

"And stop following me," she said. "Christ, you're like a little yappy dog."

She went inside.

I heard cawing. I saw a black crow disappear into the field. I knew it must be up to no good. Crows are criminals. They break into brains and steal secrets and spread garbage all over the street. Then another one came. Now two more. I couldn't see what they were doing but I didn't like it one bit. I went in the house to put on my spy clothes.

I snuck out to where the crows were. I kept my hands up around my face and looked through my fingers because I wanted to be ready to cover up in case any of them attacked. One look into my eyes and they would know all about Ada and Miles and Jody and I was afraid of who they might go chirp to. Maybe the cops. Worse, maybe Mum. As I got closer the cawing got louder. There were a bunch of them circling high above, keeping an eye out for me. But I was such a good spy I went undetected. Soon I saw what they were doing.

Since the two people on my street who owned shovels wouldn't talk to me anymore, Georgina because she said wherever I went trouble followed and Winston because he caught me feeding his pigs a meal of garbage, I could no longer bury things. Instead I had to cover my secrets with a pile of dirt and grass and the crows were using their beaks to try and uncover them. This was their revenge. Mum once said something about a murder of crows. That was my doing. But I didn't know what I did to make the green flies so angry. There were hundreds of them. They were buzzing mad and helping out the crows.

Right away I knew this was war and I needed weapons.

Mum was back out on the step, smoking, her yellow hair blowing in the wind.

"You've been spending a lot of time out there lately," she said.

I got quiet and watched her watch me.

"What, you don't got anything to say for yourself?"

"Does this mean you're talking to me again?"

"Just because I asked you a question doesn't mean that you're in my good books."

"I didn't know you had good books."

"That's probably because you're never in them."

"So how do I get in them?"

"You can start by telling me what's out there?"

"Crows and green flies."

"I can see that, Einstein. I mean, what are they doing out there?"

I didn't know what to say. I wanted to get in Mum's good books but I knew I wouldn't stay in them for long if I told her what the crows and green flies were doing. I was still trying to think of something to say when Mum said she was going to go have a look.

"No," I said. "Somebody left their garbage out there. That's all."

"Way out there?"

"Yeah."

Mum sucked on her cigarette.

"You're hiding something," she said, smoke escaping from her mouth.

I was sweaty and scared but I smiled to fool her.

"Don't smile at me. His car is here, his bag is here. Christ, he couldn't have gone far. I know you know something. Just tell me the truth."

"I'm glad Jody's gone. I didn't like him one bit."

Mum was shaking now. Her eyes were like mud puddles and she dropped her cigarette on the ground. She crushed it with her bare foot and went inside.

Soon I was sneaking back across the field with two grocery bags full of rocks and a steak knife in my pocket, just in case. When I was close enough to be able to hit the crows with rocks I dropped my bags. I crouched on the ground and spied through my fingers. I saw a sneaker and a white sock and an arm and some of them were perched on it like it was a tree branch and they were stabbing it with their beaks, eating the hair and skin. They were even eating the smelly sock, which proved to me that crows would eat anything like Winston's pigs.

I was dizzy and sweating and so far war was a lot like getting one of Georgina's special hugs, right down to the tingling in my bum and belly. I liked war. I thought maybe I could be a spy in a war when I grew up. I grabbed a rock. I covered my eyes with my other arm to protect my brain and started throwing.

There were rocks flying through the air like bullets and crows and flies being shot as they ate their dinner and broken beaks and wings and blood and cawing and buzzing and falling and flapping to get back up and attack and the rocks kept coming and some of the crows and flies got away but some of them didn't.

When I ran out of rocks I waited, listening. All I heard was my breathing and I uncovered my eyes.

There was one crow wiggling on the ground like a worm and I ran up to it and before its black beady eyes could break into my brain I took the steak knife from my pocket and stabbed it in the neck. Blood poured out onto the ground and it was thick and dark like pancake syrup and my belly grumbled. I was hungry after all this war and I thought about Jody's bologna. It was hiding under my pillow and there was still some of it left.

I was happy that I had won the war and smiled thinking about my murders. I hoped that all the crows and flies were already eating stinky garbage from some giant stinky dump in the ground and Jody was there with them eating plastic and Styrofoam and egg shells because he was one of them all right. And I hoped Miles was somewhere else. That he was with all the good people like his mum and Ada and Lily, up in the sky close to the sun where it was always summer.

And then I saw Mum. She was standing in the field, staring at the pile of grass and dirt.

I waited for her to talk, my heart pounding quick and loud like a rap song.

A dog barked.

A clothesline squeaked.

The wind was blowing my hair and the field and I thought I could feel rain.

Mum was shaking like it was the middle of winter and she was outside without her coat. She knew what I'd done. I didn't know what would happen next. The police officer might come and ask more questions that scared Mum. I might go to the same jail as my dad. Maybe Mum would be glad that it was just me and her again and we would go on living in Jody's house, that would be the happiest ending I could ever hope for. I waited to see what she'd say.

It's been years. I've had so many birthdays I've lost count and I'm still waiting for Mum to say something.

AUTHOR BIOGRAPHY

Keir Lowther lives in Prince Edward Island with his wife, daughter and dog. His great grandfather was Lucy Maud Montgomery's first cousin.

ACKNOWLEDGEMENTS

To Robin, who is my wife, best friend, my sous chef, mother of my children, and first editor.

To William Kowalski, who is my mentor, friend and second editor.

To those who saw potential in me and this book—Shaun Bradley (agent extraordinaire), Shirarose Wilensky, and the Writers' Federation of Nova Scotia.

To Robyn Read (editor) for really getting this book and Nathaniel G. Moore and the folks at Tightrope for really getting behind it.

And to the rest of you, including those two crazy kids who conceived me back in the summer of 1977, thank you thank you thank you.

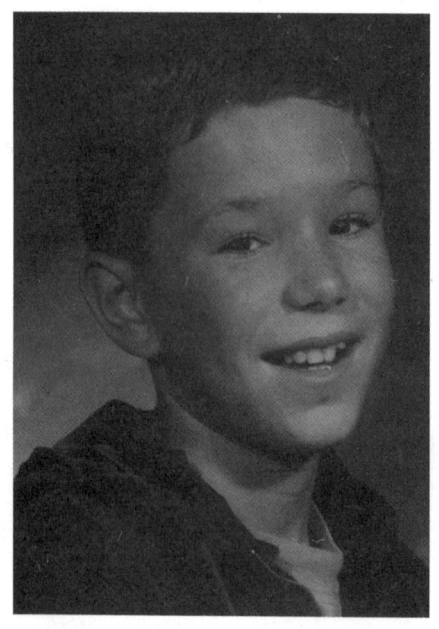

In Memory of Morgan Dane MacPhail
December 14, 1978 – December 22, 2002